Two Skeletons; One Closet

TR CLIBORNE

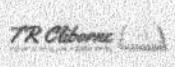

# TWO SKELETONS; ONE CLOSET

CONTENTS

For Murch,
You were the best fur companion anyone could ask for.
You kept all my secrets, loved me like no other
and will forever be the goodest boy.
I will miss you always.

PROLOGUE

She was only trying to help; she shouldn't have touched his things or gone into that room. If she were being honest, she hated that room. She didn't know why she had gone in there. Yes, she did; she wanted to please him, to help him. Uncle was always in such a good mood when he was pleased.

She hated when Uncle took her picture. It always meant a "friend" would come by soon. She hated Uncle's friends; they made her cry. She learned early on that crying only made things worse. Sometimes his "friends" would hurt her, or they would tell Uncle she was trouble, and he would lock her in her room for a long time. If she didn't do well in front of the camera, she thought Uncle's friends would not want to meet her. It was a stupid child's way of thinking. Now that she was nearly 13, she knew better. The longer it took to get a good picture, the longer the isolation, the longer the silent treatment, the longer she went without seeing her cousins.

She had many cousins. They never stayed long, not like her. She had been with Uncle for as long as she could remember. She came to stay with him when her parents had gone away. She was barely six and scared. At first, she was confused; her parents had said nothing about leaving, and she had never met her uncle until he picked her up that day. In the beginning, he tolerated her crying and questions.

After a while, he simply ignored her, then he became angry, saying things like, "Isn't it enough that I take care of you when they asked?" "Do I not feed and clothe you out of my pocket?"

Uncle would call her ungrateful, a burden, or even greedy. Uncle said schools were full of people who wanted to hurt her, teachers who knew nothing about what they taught, and other children who would make fun of her. That is why he said he would teach her at home. When she was almost eight, Uncle said the police had called to say a car accident had killed her parents. There had been no funeral because of how bad the accident had been. Uncle was all she had after that. There was no more hope of going home. Her only hope was to please him, to keep him happy.

That made her go into the room that day. One of her cousins had been crying when Uncle was trying to get an excellent picture. He had been so upset. There were a few cousins staying with them, and that always made him stressed out. There were seldom good days when the house was full. She felt awful when she heard her cousins cry out; she knew their pain, but more so, she needed Uncle to be happy.

That day she had overseen breakfast for herself and her cousins. Uncle had to run a few errands early and left her in charge. The small area constructed for them was bare; the kitchen had a small refrigerator, a hot plate, and a few dishes. She made them scrambled eggs and toast with milk. After she had set out the crayons and paper while she cleaned up. She didn't mind because she knew it would please Uncle that this minor task was complete when he returned. That made her smile. There were no windows in the small area, so she wasn't sure what time of day it was, just the small clock on the wall that Uncle put up when he taught her to tell time hinted at hours that passed.

She had been sweeping when she noticed the lock on the picture room had not been pushed closed. At first, she panicked, thinking Uncle might be trying to trick her. He had done that before. But no, not with the picture room; he would never do that on purpose. Uncle was very careful with that room. Only he and one cousin at a time were permitted in there. No one was to disturb him, no matter what was heard, while he was in there. He had been so angry yesterday when he could not get a decent picture of her young cousin. She had her picture taken so many times that she knew how the camera worked. She hated that room, how it made her feel to have her picture taken; she could almost taste the bile coming up thinking about it. More so, she needed Uncle to be happy.

That need, that instinct for survival, is why she went in there. Everything was set up for pictures still. She knew she should not be in there; she knew what taking the pictures would mean for her cousin, and it pained her. She also knew what it would mean if Uncle couldn't get the pictures he needed again; that terrified her. She had to try; this was her chance to prove she wasn't ungrateful, that she could be of use in any other way than he was using her.

She put on her most cheerful smile and went back to where her cousins were arguing over a blue crayon. She pretended to be in awe of their artwork, telling them she would ask Uncle for tape to put the drawings on the wall if they finished without more arguing. That seemed to quiet them some. She grabbed a brush and did her hair in braids; Uncle liked braids, but she had another reason for them today. When she returned, she brought the brush and asked if anyone else would like some braids too. She looked at her youngest cousin, who sat quietly in a corner alone. The small girl wasn't crying anymore, which was good.

She approached the girl cautiously, trying to keep her smile big and her voice light. She sat next to the girl and said nothing for a bit. She just sat next to her, trying to find the right words. She needed to speak carefully if this was going to work.

The girl finally looked down at the floor and asked, "When is my mommy coming?"

It was the "in" she needed. She should comfort the girl the way she needed to be comforted so many years ago, but more so, she needed to please Uncle.

"I'm not sure, little one, but crying in the corner won't make the time go any faster." She thought she could see tears welling in the girl's eyes again, so she quickly added, "How about we play a game to pass the time, just us?"

This seemed to pique the girl's interest some. She quickly went on, "I love playing princesses. We can do your hair and then get some dress-up clothes, just us. You can be the princess this time since you are new here. Would you like that?"

The girl almost smiled as she looked up at her. She knew that would work. She put the girl's hair in two perfect French braids. Then she led the girl into the picture room and shut the door.

The girl was frightened when the door closed, but she calmed quickly when she said, "You don't want the others to see what we are up to, do you?"

They went through the trunk of costumes until they had found a pretty ballerina leotard with a matching tutu. There was even a small tiara to finish the outfit nicely. By then, the girl was giggling and at ease. They set up the background and found some props.

They played for a bit before she said, "You look so royal. I should take a picture for you to give your mommy later!"

The little girl loved this idea and posed with ease.

She turned on the camera and figured out which buttons to push, even playing with the lighting. As much as she hated being on the other side of the camera, she loved being on this side. The world seemed so different from here. She forgot what all this meant, what came next. She started snapping pictures, capturing the true happiness in the small girl's smile. She felt at home.

It wasn't until she heard another argument and crash that she came out of her dream state behind the lens. She told the girl to get dressed and put everything away so they would not get into trouble. Then she went out to see what was going on. The others had broken several crayons, and a drawing lay torn on the floor. She glanced at the clock and panicked when she realized how many hours had gone by.

"What have you done? Get this cleaned up now!" She began flying around the small space, picking things up, putting things away.

She barely realized she was shaking. She heard Uncle coming and told the others to go to their rooms. She quickly checked the picture room to make sure it was back the way it should be before going to her room. She sat on the bed, tugging at her hair, trying to keep the fear from taking over.

"Who the hell has been in this room?" Uncle growled from outside her door.

How did he know? The door! She forgot to close the door! She could hear him stomping through the picture room, muttering under his breath. He must have realized he had not closed the lock. Then it got quiet.

The quiet scared her more than the yelling. In the quiet, you could hear your own thoughts running rampant, your nightmares turning into reality. She didn't even realize she had been stroking the small scar on the top of her shoulder where Uncle had burned her one night when one of his friends had complained. It hurt so badly for a long time, but she didn't even notice it anymore. It healed into a small mark that looked like half a heart. Uncle told her that was because when she was bad, it broke his heart to punish her.

The doorknob turned slowly, and she braced herself for her punishment. She knew it would be harsh, and she suddenly hated her little cousin. Why had she made her go in there? Why couldn't she have just taken the pictures with Uncle yesterday? She could feel him looking at her even with her eyes closed.

Uncle asked in an unusual tone, "Did you take these?"

In almost a whisper, she replied, "Yes..."

The door closed again before she could mutter an apology. She was confused about what had just transpired. She began to weep until she had cried herself to sleep.

She woke sometime later; she assumed the next day since she could hear her cousins laughing in the common space. Uncle was cooking, which was unusual. Her eyes were still swollen from her tears, and she rubbed them to bring her vision into focus as she sat up. There on the floor was a box, wrapped in pretty paper, tied with a red ribbon. She slowly reached for the box, looking it over.

In fine print was simple lettering that said, "To: My Special Girl From: Uncle." She tore through the paper and opened the box.

Uncle had given her a camera of her own. She had pleased him.

| 1 |

CHAPTER 1

SUMMER, 2008

This summer was the hottest Shane could remember. Sweat was pouring out of him faster than he could gulp down his Gatorade. Florida summers were miserable and unpredictable. One minute the sun was beating down on you, the air so thick it took a conscious effort to breathe. The next minute the skies were dark, clouds opening, letting the rain fall like water from a spigot. Not a mile down the road, it would be clear and dry, like a monsoon wasn't attempting to drown out every bit of life right where you stand. Shane would never get used to the bipolar summer weather.

It was so hot, the salt from his sweat was visible around his collar. He would pray for a thunderstorm if he weren't positive, one was already brewing. Camp was just about done for the day, then he just needed enough time to swing by the YMCA to pick up his sister before making a dash for the house before the skies opened. Shane hated that he was always rushing home after camp to walk his sister home from the Y. He wished he could hang out with the guys for once. Just once he yearned to cut up, grab an Icee from the corner gas station, and talk about tryouts next year.

Baseball was really all he thought about these days. When he wasn't at camp running drills, he was watching reruns of games, oiling his glove, or practicing his swing in the backyard. In the fall, he would start high school. His only chance of not being thrown to the cast-aways was to make the baseball team. He was putting every ounce of energy into being the best, the fastest, and the most agile. He didn't have the growth spurt he had hoped for and was still on the lanky side. What he lacked in height and muscle, he was making up for in speed.

His sister, Daphne, had started cheer camp at the YMCA this summer. At ten years old, she was very smart and knew how to work their parents. Shane was fourteen, and this was the first summer he was allowed to attend camp. He was so excited about baseball camp that he almost hadn't heard that he would have to go straight to the Y to walk Daph home every day. At first, he hadn't minded. Then the guys started making jokes about him being the president of the "Babysitters Club." Now it felt more like a chore than a fair trade.

The YMCA was only six blocks from their home, and Shane didn't understand why Daph couldn't make the trek on her own. The camps ended at three o'clock, and it took Shane ten minutes to get to the Y, then another ten minutes to walk the six blocks home. It seemed like such a waste of time to him. They could be home at the same time if she could just walk home herself. Shane knew she wanted too anyway.

***

Today was picture day at cheer camp, and Daphne made sure every hair was in place and plastered down with gel. She wasn't allowed to wear makeup yet, but she had allowed the photographer to put some light pink gloss on her lips. Her parents would probably think it was just the way the pictures looked and would never notice it anyway. It was just a little darker than her natural color, but it made her feel like a model.

Daph had watched the other girls as they had their photographs taken, and none of them were offered any of the shiny gloss. Daph felt special, far older than her ten years. Her cheer outfit was a perfect fit for her. The red and silver colors complemented her dark brown hair and fair skin. The lady behind the camera told her she had a face for pictures, no, that wasn't it, she used another word, something that had made her feel important. What was it she said? Photonetic? No, that wasn't it either. It didn't matter; she was having a great day, and nothing was going to spoil it.

They had taken pictures earlier in the morning before practice. Daph was glad about that because by lunch, her hair was poking out at the sides. The gloss had long worn off, and she was sweating. The gym at the Y had large fans running, and the doors were open, but the heat was sticky and the air thick. There were only two more hours left before camp would let out for the day. Daph would wait under the awning with the others until her brother Shane came from baseball camp to walk her home. She didn't understand why she had to wait for him. She never waited long, but she felt like such a child doing so.

The photographer stuck around to get candid shots of them practicing throughout the afternoon. Daphne wanted to look pretty in the pictures, so she made a dash for the small dressing rooms when she finished eating. There were bathrooms in there where she could fix her hair with the small comb she had shoved in her bag. There were two other girls in there already, so Daph went to the bathroom first.

When she heard the giggling girls fading away, she came out of the stall and made her way to a small counter in front of a wide mirror. She tried to comb her flyaways back into place, but all the gel she had used had made her hair stiff and unmanageable.

She was about to give up when she heard a voice say, "Would you like some help?"

Daph looked up to see the strange lady staring back at her in the mirror. She must have looked startled because the lady quickly followed with, "I didn't mean to scare you; I thought you saw me. I used to do my sister's hair all the time, is all. I can help if you want."

It took a second for Daphne to realize who the lady was. She didn't want her to think she was some scaredy-cat kindergartner.

Daphne plastered a wide smile on her face. "You didn't scare me. I just thought I was alone, that's all."

Daph handed her the comb and watched through the mirror as the lady went to the sink and wet the comb. She came back and effortlessly put the hair back in place. Then, she reached into her oversized bag and pulled out a small can of spray.

"It's just a little hairspray. You know what that is, right?"

Daphne nodded her head and closed her eyes as the lady sprayed her head. After the lady was finished, Daphne opened her eyes and thanked the lady.

Daphne watched the lady grab her things and walk away.

She was just about out of sight before she turned back and said, "Daphne, is it?" Again, she nodded her head, and the lady continued, "You really are very photogenic. How old are you? About thirteen?"

Daphne smiled and let out a quiet laugh. "I'm ten and a half."

The lady put a hand to her chest in shock, "Wow, I would have never thought. It was very nice to meet you, Daphne, ten and a half." Then, with a wink, she turned and left.

Photogenic- that was the word! Daphne wasn't sure what that meant, but it sounded awesome. She grabbed her things and joined the rest of the group, who were lining up for drills on the blue mats that lined the center of the gym. The rest of the afternoon passed in a swirl of red and silver, spinning, twirling, and jumping, almost as fast as Daphne's heart.

***

Shane was packing up his gear when he heard the guys talking about grabbing a slice of pizza. He wished he could go with them and wondered if they would even bother to ask him. At the start of camp, they invited him a lot, but he always had to turn them down to rush off to the Y in time to meet Daph. The pizza shop was on the way to the Y, so maybe this time he could go. It would take two minutes to walk that way and order a slice. No one would even know that he hadn't gone straight to the Y. It was just once. Once he got to act like a teenager. Even as he thought it, he knew it was wrong, but he had already decided that he would say yes this time.

He took his time packing his gear, even pulling things out and putting them back in. At one point, Shane dropped his bat on purpose to let the guys know he was still there. They barely paused in their conversation, though, before heading off. Shane had become almost invisible to them now. He didn't blame them; there are only so many times a guy can say no before you stopped asking. It had taken an extra five minutes to get his things back in his bag. He glanced at his watch before setting course for the Y; he was already running late, but he didn't care today.

They hadn't even asked him this time. Shane was fuming. He knew it was childish, and his slower than usual pace was intentional at this point. Shane was tired, sore, hungry, and he felt slighted. It wasn't Daphne's fault, but he couldn't stop the anger he felt swelling in his chest. When did it become his responsibility to take care of his sister? He was almost an adult! He was fourteen, almost a freshman in high school, and instead of enjoying pizza with the guys, he was off to fill his role as president of the "Babysitters Club."

Just then, as if sensing the shift in his mood, the sun disappeared behind a dark cloud, and a loud clap of thunder sounded overhead. Normally, the warning of a thunderstorm would have Shane setting into a trot, but not today. He wasn't in the mood. If he was going to get drenched, so was Daphne.

***

Where was Shane? Daphne didn't have a watch, but she knew Shane was late. All the other girls had left or picked up already. She was never the last one. She craned her head as much as she could to see down the sidewalk, looking for Shane to come running around the corner. However, there was no one in sight. Daphne let out a sigh and was about to do a cartwheel when the sky grew dark, and a loud rumble crashed in the sky.

Daphne had such a great day; she wasn't about to let anyone spoil it. She could walk home by herself. If she left now and took the shortcut, she would make it home before the rain started. She didn't have her own house key, but she could wait on the porch or slip through the bathroom window she knew her mom never locked. Shane would not ruin her day.

"Isn't your brother coming today?" Her coach's voice broke through her thoughts.

Daphne stopped for a second, then blurted, "Oh my! I forgot; I was supposed to walk home with Chelsea today."

The coach asked if she should call her mom, but Daphne took the opportunity to run off, yelling behind her, "No need, I should hurry before the rain."

Daphne felt so free! Could this day really get any better? She ran the two blocks, then quickly looked around before hitting the shortcut that ran behind her neighborhood, coming out just before her street. Shane had shown her this route a few times when they had gotten stuck in the rain, and Daphne knew it well. Her mom would be so mad if she knew Daphne had gone this way. She was always telling them to stay on the sidewalk, not to talk to strangers, and to go straight home. Daphne didn't understand all the fuss. They had lived here forever, and nothing bad ever happened. Well, nothing that she had ever heard about anyway.

Daphne was halfway down the trail when the sky suddenly burst open, and the rain started coming from all directions. She ran for what seemed like ages; sure, she had missed the turn that opened onto the street just before hers. It was raining so hard that it was impossible to see anything. Daphne kept going; she knew that there were only two exits, and both would bring her to her neighborhood even if she missed one.

***

Shane was just making his way up the path when the rain started. He knew something was wrong before he even made his way up the path. No one was standing under the awning waiting. He knew he was a little late, but only by ten minutes. Someone should still be there with Daph. A quick glance at the parking lot told him he was alone even before he reached the gym doors. They were locked tight, and no one was going to answer, but Shane pounded on them anyway.

After a few minutes, he started yelling for Daphne, but only his echo answered. Maybe his mom picked her up because of the storm, or maybe she had gotten sick? This thought fueled the anger that had started earlier. If Daphne had been picked up and no one thought to swing by to tell him, he would never let them forget. Not only did he have to pass up hanging out with his friends, but now he was getting soaked walking home when the princess had gotten a ride?

Shane was pretty sure there was no scenario where this was fair. He had given up his summer to watch Daphne, and no one could give him a thought. He would make a fuss about this, maybe even get a pack of baseball cards out of it.

He knew his parents already felt bad asking him to watch Daphne over the summer, so he could get something out of this. His trouble should be rewarded after all.

Even through his anger, a feeling he couldn't describe was welling in the pit of his stomach. He tried to push it down with thoughts of ways he could use this to his advantage. But the closer he got to home, the stronger the feeling got. Daphne almost always got her way. Their parents doted on her in a way they had never done with him. However, his dad always took time to sneak into his room after Daphne went to bed to ask him about his day. His mom always made sure his uniform was ready and clean next to the lunch she made him.

Deep down, where this feeling was growing stronger, he knew they wouldn't have forgotten to tell him; they would not have left him. A thought that was confirmed when he turned the corner to see his driveway empty. Shane was in a full sprint before he knew it, fumbling with the key, then the lock, before swinging the door wide open, screaming for his sister.

| 2 |

CHAPTER 2

CRANE, JANUARY 2022

Crane reluctantly roused herself from the haze of sleep, her eyes still heavy with drowsiness. The room was cloaked in darkness, adding to her confusion as she couldn't recall the events leading up to her slumber. It was like a puzzle missing crucial pieces. Just as she was piecing together the fragments of her memory, her alarm shattered the silence, jolting her into reality. With a mix of resignation and annoyance, she muttered to herself and her loyal companion, K9 Murch, who lay beside her on the bed, emitting a sympathetic groan.

Muffling the obnoxious honking of her phone, Crane embarked on her weekday ritual, stumbling through her cramped room towards the minuscule kitchen. She fumbled to start the coffeepot, its familiar aroma promising solace amid her morning fog. Opening the back door, she allowed Murch to venture into the world outside, ensuring he was well-fed before returning to her room. Suppressing the temptation to surrender to the allure of her cozy bed, she hastily donned a pair of sweats and grabbed her sneakers.

As Crane savored the invigorating elixir of her first cup of coffee, she found Murch eagerly awaiting their daily run by the door. Plugging in her headphones and queuing up a captivating podcast, she set off on her familiar route through the neighborhood, which was still shrouded in the predawn darkness. The scattered houses in the new development blinked with only a few lights, as if the world was still lost in slumber. Crane's mother had celebrated her decision to purchase the 1600 sq ft split plan, proclaiming it as a sign of putting down roots. Even though she knew Crane had never strayed far from the place she called home since childhood, never venturing over fifteen minutes away.

Crane's morning runs were like a voyage into her own thoughts, but she remained vigilant of her surroundings. The gentle tug on her leash brought her back to reality as she realized she had returned to her starting point - home. She had developed a habit of observing everything, whether it was the idling blue car two streets away, the flickering porch light at Mrs. Carter's house half a mile down the road, or the bent post in the fence that the kids used as a shortcut to the bus stop. Even on her runs, her subconscious mind made sure she didn't miss a thing.

Today, Crane had gone farther than usual, and a quick glance at the clock confirmed she was running late. Murch, her loyal companion, curled up on her pillow as she proceeded to the shower with her second cup of coffee. The hot water cascaded over her tired muscles, providing a brief respite before she emerged into the hazy bathroom. She stepped onto the cool floor, realizing that even in the heart of winter, Florida's temperatures rarely dipped below a comfortable sixty degrees. In this part of the world, seasons were merely variations of wet summer and dry summer.

As Crane settled behind the wheel of her car, she knew she was already twenty minutes behind schedule. It bothered her, despite the fact that she would still be the first one in the office, arriving an hour before everyone else. The thought of hitting the highway at seven didn't sit well with her - school buses and never-ending rush hour would only add another fifteen minutes to her commute.

Crane was just about to savor her third cup of coffee when a monstrous truck with oversized tires and a bold "FLOGROWN" sticker on the window suddenly swerved into her lane. Startled, she slammed on the brakes, causing the scalding hot coffee to splash onto her lips and spill all over her lap. "Son of a bi...," Crane managed to catch herself before honking the horn, opting instead to smack the top of the steering wheel in frustration. If she had been in her personal vehicle, she would have unleashed a barrage of obscenities at the truck. Hitting the horn in her city vehicle meant activating the siren in the unmarked cruiser, attention she did not need. So, she simply shook her head in disbelief and muttered something about turn signals and the driver's ego.

As Crane approached the entrance gate of the PD headquarters, she swiped her access card with a sense of relief. Glancing at the clock on the dashboard, she noted it was only twenty minutes past seven, not too bad considering the delayed start to her day. Finding a parking spot towards the back, she reached for her phone in the cradle. As she scrolled through a few work emails, searching for any intriguing crime bulletins, her phone suddenly rang, interrupting her concentration. Without even needing to glance at the caller ID, Crane knew it was her mother. No one else would dare call her this early on a Monday morning. Ever since her father's passing two years ago, it had become a weekly ritual.

With forced cheeriness, Crane answered the call, juggling her belongings as she made her way towards the building. The conversation flowed predictably, following the same pattern as every week. Her mother would inquire about her romantic life, making sure she was getting enough rest and nourishment, and of course, sharing the latest gossip about someone's son who had recently gone through a divorce. Finding Crane a suitable partner before her thirtieth birthday next year had become her mother's personal mission. It didn't matter that Crane had no interest in settling down or that she was content with her thriving career.

"What was that? Mom? I'm going to lose you in the elevator, I'll call you tonight. Love you."

Crane didn't wait for an answer before hanging up. If it were important, she would get a string of text messages by the time she reached her desk. Crane used the term "important" very loosely. The urgent text messages could range from a death in the family to Mr. Tomkins cat riling up her sweet tabby, Gigi.

Moving down the silent hallway, Crane activated the motion-sensing lights as she went. She passed by numerous glass doors that revealed larger rooms filled with cubicles, soon to be bustling with dedicated detectives tirelessly working to solve an array of crimes. In her seven years as a police officer, Crane had experienced almost every beat and shift imaginable during her time in patrol. Along the way, she had earned a coveted position on the Special Victims Response Team, allowing her to work alongside seasoned detectives while still on patrol. With television shows glamorizing working as detectives in specialized units, being able to be a part of that world was an amazing experience for new officers. Openings on the team were few and far between. After four years, she had earned the title of detective in the Property division before moving on to Auto Theft and Economic Crimes.

Finally, Crane arrived at a sturdy wooden door equipped with a key lock and a proxy access point. She swiftly scanned her ID and unlocked the door with her key. As it closed behind her, enveloping the room in darkness, Crane wasted no time. With one hand, she dropped her bag next to a desk adorned with multiple large computer screens. With the other hand, she began the process of powering on the monitors. This secluded office was the only one without windows, ensuring maximum privacy, and had direct internet access independent of the department's network. Crane shared this compact space with two other detectives, Adams and Vickers, who would typically wander in around nine o'clock.

Just over a year ago, Crane found herself in the Internet Crimes Against Children (ICAC) Unit, a place that felt like home to her. The work was grueling; the hours seemed endless, and the cases never seemed to reach a satisfying conclusion. Despite the challenges, Crane knew that this work was not only necessary but also of utmost importance. The unit relied on grants from the Department of Justice, with funds being managed by the regional lead agency for various task forces. While technically part of the Special Victims Unit, Crane's team focused on investigating sex crimes against children reported through tip lines provided by the National Center for Missing and Exploited Children, ensuring that the cases were directed to the appropriate jurisdiction.

In a single day, Crane witnessed more child sexual abuse material (CSAM) than most of the criminals she arrested had seen in their entire lives. Each flagged video and photograph had to be meticulously examined, searching for any clue that could help identify the individuals involved and enable Crane to provide factual testimony in court. Much of what she encountered were adults, some appearing to be past puberty, making it impossible to confirm their ages as minors. There were also instances of child erotica, which, although disturbing, did not fall under illegal content. However, it was the truly disturbing videos that haunted Crane's thoughts, the kind that would send shivers down anyone's spine and linger long after watching. These were the images that brought the boogeyman to life. It was these videos and their innocent victims that fueled Crane's determination.

Before settling at her desk, Crane made a pot of coffee. As she looked around the room, she saw a wall covered with pictures of victims who had been identified and rescued from the horrors depicted in those videos. Each image represented a child who had been saved from their living nightmare. On another wall, Crane had placed photographs of her parents, herself, and her sister, and two additional pictures. These last two were computer-generated age progression images, depicting how two girls who had haunted Crane's thoughts her whole life might look now. These were two girls who were out there, forgotten by everyone else, but not by Crane.

Crane eagerly clicked open multiple chat boxes, each representing a different app, scattered across her various screens. With a sense of anticipation, she logged into the ICAC portal, ready to delve into the new tips that had accumulated over the weekend. As she patiently waited for the information to load, Crane took a moment to refuel, pouring herself the fourth cup of coffee for the day.

Sitting back down at her desk, she plugged in her headphones, immersing herself in the task at hand. Her eyes scanned the tally displayed before her, revealing an astounding one hundred and fifty-seven fresh tips.

A wry smile tugged at the corners of her lips as she muttered to herself, "Happy Monday, welcome to Florida, the human trafficker's paradise."

| 3 |

CHAPTER 3

WINTER, 2009

Vanessa sat on her freshly made bed, waiting to hear any movement from her sister's room. Usually, she wouldn't be up and ready so early during winter break, but today was no ordinary Tuesday. Her ballet studio had been rehearsing for a special Christmas Eve performance of "The Nutcracker" for the last month. Until yesterday, Vanessa had a supporting role. Her leotard and tutu were so beautiful, and she knew her routine by heart, which was exciting enough. Last night, however, her instructor called with the best news ever: Lisa, who had the lead role of the Sugarplum Fairy, had to drop out due to her grandmother passing away. The family had to drive to South Carolina and would not be returning until after the New Year. Mrs. Blanchard asked her to fill in for Lisa!! It was the greatest thing to happen to Vanessa in all her eleven years. Not the part about Lisa's grandma, that was awful, but Vanessa had to take opportunities when they came.

Vanessa was tall and slender with dark brown hair, all the physical traits of a prima ballerina. However, where God blessed her physically, he bypassed her with grace. Vanessa knew she lacked the coordination Lisa had, but she had practiced alongside her, memorizing not only her part but Lisa's as well. Today she had to look her best for her fitting of the new costume and photograph for the program that will be handed out the night of the show. It is just a paper printed off by Mrs. Blanchard, but it would have her picture on the front! The recital was going to be held during the Christmas Eve festival downtown. They were using the stage by the lake, and the whole town would be there. Vanessa was so excited she had a bruise on her forearm from pinching herself.

That is why today was so important; she had to look her best. Most days, she did all she could to avoid her sister. Abigail was sixteen, with the same tall, slim figure and dark hair as Vanessa. Their father said they looked like carbon copies of their mother, which Vanessa loved hearing. Their mom had been a ballerina when she was younger. Not a prima ballerina like Vanessa wanted to be, but she had danced for a small production company through college. Abigail had no interest in dancing. Abigail was a straight-A student with eyes on politics and boys. Most days, it seemed like they had been copy and pasted from a mold but given entirely unique programming.

Abigail had one talent Vanessa envied: makeup. Vanessa often watched in awe as Abigail used her brushes to paint her face with swirls of color that made her porcelain skin radiant. It was an art that Vanessa hoped to learn when she was older. At eleven, her mother did not allow her to possess makeup, let alone wear it unless it was for a performance. Even then, her mom would throw on a little blush, some sparkling shadow, and tinted gloss. It made her look like a doll. Today, Vanessa needed perfection; she needed Abigail.

Vanessa woke early, dressed, and put her hair in a perfect bun. Now she sat nervously waiting to hear Abigail moving about so she could beg her on hands and knees if needed to do her makeup. She knew it would take convincing since Abigail already saw her as an inconvenience. Abigail complained all the time about having to drive Vanessa around, saying she felt like a chauffeur, or that Vanessa was always impeding her social commitments, whatever that meant. Today it didn't matter; Vanessa would do whatever it took to win her sister over, even tattling. A girl's got to do what a girl's got to do, right?

Vanessa heard movement from across the hall, and she prepared herself. The door to her sister's room opened, and a few seconds later, a half-awake Abigail appeared. She must have sensed Vanessa staring because she looked up, still trying to rub the sleep from her eyes.

"Aren't you just the Peppy Nessie?"

Vanessa hated being called Nessie, a nickname she had since she could remember. It reminded her of the Loch Ness Monster, not at all fitting for a ballerina.

"Today is the fitting for my recital, and Mrs. Blanchard is having my picture taken for the program," Vanessa blurted out.

Abigail just stared at her as if there should be a more significant reason for Vanessa's excitement. Vanessa quickly went on before losing her nerve.

"It's a really important day. The program will be handed out to everyone on Christmas Eve, and I want to look my best. I was wondering if, I mean if I could do something for you if..." Abigail cut her stammering off.

"For Christ's sake, Ness, what do you want?"

Vanessa resisted the urge to roll her eyes, instead gripping the side of the bed tightly before asking, "Abbs, would you pretty please do my makeup?"

Abigail didn't move or say anything, and Vanessa wasn't sure she heard her at first.

Then she let out a light laugh before saying, "No amount of makeup is going to conceal your lack of talent, little one."

Vanessa knew not to take the bait, but the words came out before she could stop them.

"Why are you always such a witch, Abigail?"

Vanessa could feel the heat rising to her face. In one quick movement, she was off the bed and slamming the door. She could still hear Abigail laughing down the hall.

When she was sure she heard the shower start, Vanessa made her way into Abigail's room. She stared at all the brushes and color palettes, not sure where to start. She had watched her sister enough to have a general idea of what to do, so she hurriedly got to work. By the time the shower cut off, Vanessa had added blush, eyeshadow, mascara, and thrown a pink lipstick into her bag. It wasn't the work of art she had hoped for, but it would do.

***

It was a quarter after two, and Abigail was pulling up to the dance studio. She knew Nessie would be all too ready to report back to Mom that she had been late again. After this morning, she didn't care though. It was bad enough that Nessie went into her room without permission, used her makeup when she knew she wasn't allowed to, but then her mother had chastised her like she was a child.

Somehow, Nessie had done everything she wasn't supposed to, but Abigail was the one who had gotten the lecture. It always seemed to go this way. Her parents both worked full time, and while they lived comfortably, they were far from rich. Her father would joke that they were one good hurricane away from being blown from the lower middle class to the upper lower class.

When Abigail turned sixteen, it came as no surprise that the older Nissan Altima and cellphone she had gotten for her birthday had come with strings attached, and not just the pretty ribbon that had been wrapped around the box containing the phone and keys. No, this present came with puppet strings.

"We are giving you the freedom of the road and instant communication so we can tie you to our endless text messages regarding your sister's schedule and gas money for your taxi services," they said.

She should be out shopping with her friends right now instead of rushing off to pick up Nessie from ballet.

It was just another string being manipulated by the marionettes that were her parents. This morning, she was reminded that she had the privilege of a driver's license because they allowed her to, because Abigail had promised to help with Ness. In all fairness, she had made that promise, but she would have said anything for a car and phone. It was as if being an honor student, class treasurer, and top writer on the school paper was not enough to be rewarded on their own merit. Her parents overlooked all her hard work and accomplishments as much as they argued they didn't.

Abigail's mom told her she was very proud of her, but as the oldest, she needed her too. She was always telling Abigail things like, "this is temporary, soon you will be off to college," or "one day you will regret not appreciating this time with your sister," or the favorite, "I wish things were different, but one day when you have a family of your own, you will understand." There was no way Abigail was ruining her life with kids. She had plans, great plans, and none of them included children.

She felt the vibration of her phone in her pocket. She didn't have to look at it to know it was her mom checking in. The text would read something like, "Hey, just making sure you and Ness are okay."

Mother's subtle way of making sure Abigail hadn't forgotten to pick up the annoying rugrat. Abigail ignored the buzzing and looked through the glass window, searching for the tall brown bun that was usually waiting by the door. Ness was taller than the rest of the girls in her class, with Lisa coming in a close second. Lisa was blonde, however, and was glued to her overbearing mother, who stayed through every rehearsal. Abigail knew Lisa was out of town, though. That is why Nessie had been so excited. She picked to take Lisa's place when she had to drop out at the last minute. Nessie had been so excited, but Abigail couldn't pass up the chance to knock the princess down a few pegs by reminding her the only reason she was given the part was that she was the only one who could fit into the costume with only three days left until the performance.

Abigail felt a pinch of guilt when she saw Ness's face on the way to the studio this morning. As mad as she had been about her getting into her stuff, she could tell Nessie was excited. In an attempt to smooth things a little, she had told her she hadn't done too bad of a job on her makeup, for a sly thief that is. Abigail was starting to get mad again when she looked at the clock, now half-past two, and still no Nessie.

"Great," she muttered as she shut the car off to go inside.

Abigail waited several minutes until Mrs. Blanchard finally appeared with a stack of papers in her hand. On the front was Nessie's smiling face perfectly posed as the Sugarplum Fairy.

Something seemed different, but Abigail quickly brushed it away when Mrs. Blanchard asked, "Abby, what can I help you with?" looking confused.

Abigail tore her eyes from the paper and looked up at Mrs. Blanchard, who seemed very puzzled to see her standing there.

"I'm here for Vanessa, Mrs. Blanchard. I didn't see her through the window. Is she in the back?"

"Vanessa was picked up already, dear. Did lines get crossed somewhere?"

At that, Abigail really began to fume. The string of vibration in her pocket made sense now. If her mother was picking Ness up early, she could have let Abigail know earlier in the day before she left her friends at lunch. It was one thing to have her carting the brat around town like she had nothing better to do, but it was another to make her cancel plans for no reason.

"Must have, thank you, Mrs. Blanchard."

Abigail was fuming by the time she got back in her car. She took a deep breath and tried to collect herself before taking out her phone. She thought about what she was going to say in response to the late text from her mother telling her she had picked up Nessie last minute. Nothing she came up with in her head didn't result in her being grounded. Abigail decided to just ignore it altogether until she had more time to cool off. She started the car and headed towards the town center. If she hurried, she could still meet up with her friends and get in some shopping.

She had just found a parking spot when her phone started vibrating again. This time, instead of a quick burst, it was continuous, indicating a call and not a text. She should just let it go to voicemail, but somehow Abigail knew that would result in losing her car privileges just as much as saying what she was thinking.

After parking the car, she pulled out her phone: four text messages, three missed calls, and one voicemail, all from her mom. Before she could even open any apps, the phone lit up again; this time it was her dad.

Abigail answered with a hesitant "hey Dad."

"Abby, thank God, where are you?" her dad spat out.

"I just pulled up to meet my friends. What's wrong?" Abigail could hear her dad let out a breath that he seemed to have been holding for a long time.

"Is Nessie with you? Did you pick her up from ballet? Have you talked to your mother?"

It all came out in such a rush that Abigail didn't know which to answer first. Normally, she would have some witty answer, but she could hear something in her father's voice. It wasn't frustration or anger; it was more like panic and desperation.

"No, Dad, Nessie isn't with me. Mrs. Blanchard told me she had already been picked up when I got there. Didn't Mom get her?"

"No, Abby, Mrs. Blanchard was worried after you showed up and called Mom. We don't know who picked Ness up. She's missing."

| 4 |

CHAPTER 4

HARRIS, JANUARY 2022

It had been an exhausting day, leaving Harris feeling famished. Despite his usual diet of grilled fish or chicken with steamed veggies, he would do anything for a mouthwatering cheeseburger dripping with grease and a refreshing Guinness. Unfortunately, none of these indulgences was within his reach for the next few weeks. Harris and his team had already spent nine days in Thailand, with several more weeks to go before returning to the States. Yet, amidst the training exercise, Harris couldn't help but appreciate the unique charm of their current location.

The Thai people were a breath of fresh air. Even in the forgotten villages beyond the bustling city, they welcomed Harris and his team with open arms. Their gratitude and warmth were incomparable. Some had less than the poorest Americans, yet they smiled as if they were kings and queens, treasuring their modest possessions as if they were made of pure gold. It didn't matter who you were or what you looked like; they embraced you wholeheartedly. Harris couldn't help but envy their genuine contentment. Living with so little, by Western standards at least, and finding joy in each day was a force stronger than any weapon forged.

The weather was nice, eighty-seven and sunny today. Back home, or in Washington, where he had been stationed for the last few years, the ground would be wet and slushy. It was a beautiful state with gorgeous trails, but the cold had a way of seeping into your bones. Living off base had its perks, but it took fifteen minutes to warm his vehicle before his 0430 departure each morning. Washington life was quite a contrast to his Florida upbringing but being chosen to attend just the Army Special Forces Assessment and Selection process out of the hundreds that dropped packets, let alone being picked up, was an honor and a dream since he signed the dotted line in the local recruiter's office back home.

The training had been grueling, but fortunately, Harris had always been athletic and had been preparing for military life since his senior year. Despite having the option to choose any job with his impressive Armed Services Vocational Aptitude Battery scores, Harris opted for the infantry.

"Infantry is a man's choice," his recruiter had told him, and it was the first unit shipping out, which suited Harris just fine.

All he could think about was creating distance between himself and the haunting memories of home. Although the sign-on bonus for infantry was meager compared to other jobs, Harris knew it would keep him on the move and open doors to countless possibilities. And it did!

In June 2012, fresh out of high school, Harris couldn't fathom sitting in a college classroom discussing philosophy. With the life experiences he had, he couldn't bear to watch his family continue to deteriorate while he remained jobless. The military was the opportunity he needed—a chance to put some distance between his past mistakes and his future. It offered him invaluable skills, the opportunity to travel, a roof over his head, and food to eat. Everything else was just the icing on the cake.

That June, his recruiter drove him to the Military Entrance Processing Station in Tampa, and from there, he was on a bus headed to Fort Benning in Georgia. Over the course of twenty-two grueling weeks of One Station Unit Training, in the scorching heat of what seemed like an endless heatwave, Harris began to doubt his choices. But he persevered and forged strong bonds with his fellow trainees. Friendships had always been elusive for Harris throughout high school, but somehow, the shared physical suffering had a way of bringing scared eighteen-year-olds together. They either succeeded as one or failed as one. If one achieved something, it was because of the collective blood and sweat of all of them. And if one screwed up, it was because they weren't working as a team, and they were punished together until they learned to function as a cohesive unit. Many didn't fully grasp the lessons being taught until the end, but once they did, it stuck with them throughout their careers. They realized they were only as capable as their least capable member, and it took the encouragement and support of everyone to become better.

The world around him became a blur, rushing by at lightning speed. Airborne School at Fort Benning and Air Assault School at Fort Campbell, Kentucky, marked Harris' first intimate encounter with the Special Forces teams. The 5th group Special Forces stationed at Fort Campbell captivated him instantly. They exuded a unique confidence, not cocky but a profound awareness of their surroundings, ready for any challenge. Their synchronized training resembled the intricate gears of a clock, each piece moving in harmony to make it tick. Their eyes told stories, and their camaraderie surpassed that of family. Harris yearned for that bond, but at eighteen, he was ineligible for the coveted 18x designation in his contract. Not that it would have guaranteed his selection, but it would have eased his path to the grueling selection process.

There had been deployments to Iraq and Afghanistan, to places he couldn't pronounce. Harris volunteered for missions, attended classes, and swiftly climbed the promotion ladder. He immersed himself in every opportunity, eager to absorb knowledge like a sponge. When he became a team leader, he ensured his soldiers were fully prepared, whether they appreciated his dedication or not. Harris didn't care about popularity; all that mattered was that they returned home unscathed. With each promotion, the weight of responsibility grew. As a squad leader, he held the lives of more soldiers in his hands. He remained unwavering in his demand for rigorous training. However, fate has a way of catching up, and soon he found himself penning heart-wrenching letters to grieving mothers, fathers, sisters, and brothers. The weight of each loss clung to his soul, carving a permanent void in his heart.

Year after year, Harris made a solemn vow to remember every family affected, reaching out from whichever corner of the world he found himself in. He offered whatever comfort he could, aware that the burden of failing to protect was not new to him. The guilt of not being able to shield others had haunted him since childhood. It was a pain deeply etched into his being, intertwining with the lives of his parents. Like suffocating vines, it choked the life they were meant to have, eradicating the joy in their eyes, and extinguishing the hope in their hearts until it shattered into countless fragments.

The military provided Harris with an escape from the anguish reflected in his parents' eyes. Gone were the days of feeling the burning anger in his chest as he witnessed their surrender. The ceaseless questions had ceased, replaced by an existence consumed by trivial trinkets devoid of meaning. Harris couldn't simply forget or fill the void with material possessions. Amidst the chaos, he found solace in silence, a respite from the battles and the futile blame game. Though everyone knew the fault lay with Harris, he refused to surrender. His unwavering determination fueled his relentless search for redemption.

Several years into his military career, Harris took a leap and submitted an application for the special forces. Months later, he received the life-altering news of being selected for the grueling Special Forces Assessment and Selection process. The initial four-week ordeal pushed his body beyond its limits, challenging him in ways he never thought possible. Yet, Harris never backed down from a challenge, especially one as significant as this. While the physical trials were arduous, it was the mental challenges that truly tested the mettle of many. Harris couldn't fathom any preparation that could adequately equip him for such trials. At times, he believed he couldn't endure another day, only to be reminded that his suffering was temporary compared to the enduring pain of others. And so, he persevered and emerged triumphant.

Harris made his wish list of jobs, with Engineer Sergeant at the top of the list. He had vast knowledge of weapons already, but being responsible for tracking every weapon and all the ammo made him think of picking up brass on the range. So, Weapons Sergeant had been number two, with Communications Sergeant and Medical Sergeant being third and fourth, respectively. When it came to his wish list for Group assignment, 5th group had been at number one. He hadn't known much about the other groups, so from there he just listed them in numerical order. He chose Arabic as his preferred language because he knew that was 5th group's region, then Spanish due to already knowing some, and then he jotted down stuff from the guy next to him. Harris really hadn't paid much attention, but he wished he had. His Defense Language Aptitude Battery scores somehow made him a great candidate for one of the languages he had mindlessly listed, one of which had been Thai. How that had been possible was a mystery.

An aptitude for learning Thai landed him a spot with 1st Group Special Forces. From here, his real training began: seven weeks of course orientation, then twenty-four weeks of language and culture, thirteen weeks of small unit tactics and SERE, fourteen weeks of Engineer training, four weeks of Robin Sage, and one week of out-processing, where he finally got to wear the ever-coveted green beret. Then he was off to Joint Base Lewis-McChord (JBLM), the base for 1st group in Washington State. Had he gone to another group, maybe had to learn Spanish, it might have been easier. Being from Florida, he had no choice but to pick up a little of the language. But being a white boy from the South, Thai was a challenge. One he took on with the same determination he had done with every other challenge. He learned enough; he would never pass as native, but he could hold a decent conversation. And for anything deeper, they had their linguist.

For sixty-six grueling weeks, he pushed his body, mind, and sanity to the brink. Reflecting back, it felt as though he had watched himself from a distance, detached from reality. At times, he had to disconnect in order to endure. This wasn't the first occasion he had sealed away his emotions in a hidden compartment within, isolating himself from the outside world, just to keep moving forward. It was a skill he had honed, akin to that of a wizard wielding a mystical power. With a flick of his wand, he could twist and contort pain and discomfort, compressing them into an impenetrable box, shielded from prying eyes. This coping mechanism had carried Harris through countless trials in his life. There were moments during his upbringing when he would gaze into the mirror, only to find an empty reflection staring back at him. Survival was all that mattered.

Now, at the age of twenty-eight, Harris possessed the wisdom of someone far beyond his years. He was no longer the scrawny child who brought turmoil to his family, haunted by the lurking specter of fear around every corner. He had grown into a formidable individual, with strength, intelligence, sharpness, and a multitude of skills. He had transformed from the hunted into the hunter, constantly vigilant, scrutinizing every face, every voice, and every place he encountered. Armed with newfound knowledge and bound to his brothers by more than mere blood, his unyielding grip on hope to rectify the mistakes of his past seemed unbreakable, as if welded to his very being.

Harris knew he preferred traveling because it put miles between him and the pain that he could never shake when he was home. Even being stationed on the other side of the country didn't give him the same feeling of freedom from that guilt that he had when he was in another country, on foreign soil, a nameless face, just another stranger in the crowd.

| 5 |

CHAPTER 5

DAPHNE, JUNE 2008

The storm was worse than Daphne thought it would be. The rain was coming down hard, causing large puddles to form. Even the parts of the path that weren't underwater were slick under her cheer sneakers. The once pristine white shoes were now caked in mud, and the laces took on an unflattering brown color. It reminded Daphne of the inside of a rotten apple. She was certain she had missed the first exit that would dump her behind the houses that lined her street. Now she was stuck tromping through the mushy ground and stinging rain until she reached the end of the trail. That would bring her to the road at the end of her subdivision, and she would have to backtrack in the rain to get home.

Her mistake had cost her at least ten minutes, so Shane knew she had left without him. He would be home already, waiting to yell at her, threatening to tell Mom and Dad. He always threatened to tattle on her when she did anything she wasn't supposed to. With her shoes ruined in a way that could only happen if she took the forbidden path, it was only a matter of time before they figured it out anyway. Daphne knew she was in for it this time. Her mind was spinning, trying to find a way out, a way to blame Shane or excuse her behavior, but she was coming up with nothing.

Daphne found her way to the trail's end, fighting her way through the thick brush, trying to dodge the sludge-filled puddles the best she could. The rain was heavier now as the tree line thinned. The wind had picked up a little, making the drops sting her face. By the time she cleared the wooded area and made her way towards the houses, she was soaking wet and shivering despite the heat. The gel and hairspray that once held her hair perfectly in place were now dissolving and dripping down her face, burning her eyes. She had made a huge mistake; she knew that, and the weight of her soaked clothing only added to the weight of that decision.

She made her way between two houses she couldn't recognize. Once on the sidewalk, she paused, not sure which direction she should go. Nothing looked familiar. She knew she was in her neighborhood, as it was the only one on this side of the woods, but she just wasn't sure where. Daphne was concentrating, trying to find something that would show her the way when she first spotted the white van slowly driving up the street. She wasn't sure if it was the chill of the rain or too many after-school specials that made the goosebumps rise on her skin.

Daphne put her head down and chose the direction away from the van. She would wait until it passed to reassess her surroundings. There had been a sign on the side, but the van had been too far to read it, and the rain did not make it any easier to pick out the details. Daphne picked up her pace, trying to give the impression that she knew exactly where she was heading. She wasn't sure if the van was still driving towards her or if it had found its way into a driveway behind her. She was too scared to turn and look, but curiosity was getting the better of her. Not only that, but if she kept going and was walking in the wrong direction, she would come to a dead end soon. What would she do then? Pretend to be going into a house? Ring a doorbell? What if no one was home? Then what? Daphne strained to hear any indication that the van was still moving in her direction, but all she heard was wind and rain. She would have to look.

Daphne bent down, pretending to tie her shoe, taking the opportunity to glance between her legs at the road behind her. She took a second to mess with the muddy laces so as not to look too obvious. She took a deep breath to steady her nerves and took a quick peek. Nothing. The street was empty. Daphne let out the breath she didn't know she was holding, shaking her head at her own silliness. She stood up and looked at the houses to her right, noting the numbers above the garages. If only there were a street name or something, she might figure out where to go. She glanced at the houses to the left and right and figured if she turned around and followed the numbers as they went down, she would get closer to the front of the neighborhood where her street was.

Daphne spun on her heels and almost stumbled backwards; her breath caught in her throat. Her heart was pounding so hard she could hear it in her ears. It was all she could hear. The wind and rain had faded to a distant murmur, barely audible over the "whoosh, whoosh, whoosh" in her head. Right in front of her sat the white van, idling in the middle of the street. She hadn't seen it when she glanced back because it had been stopped right next to her. Her brain was telling her to scream, her legs wanting to run, but she stood there silent and frozen. Numb and tingling all at once. Nothing coming into focus, just a white glow in the middle of the street.

Daphne forced herself to breathe. In through her nose, out through her mouth. One deep breath, and then another. Slowly, the buzzing in her head started to subside; she no longer felt like she was going to pass out. Her eyes regained some focus, and the white glow slowly took form. First, a white box, then there were tires, a sliding door, and a picture of a camera on the door. The whoosh in her ears was replaced by the quiet sound of an engine, the swish of wipers flipping raindrops from the windshield. The window was rolled halfway down, and someone was speaking to her. A voice, calling out through a tunnel, a familiar voice, a woman's voice. None of it made any sense to her through her panic.

The voice was shouting now, and she started to register that it was calling her name.

"Daphne? That's it, right? Is that you? Are you okay?"

All of a sudden, it hit her. It was the photographer from cheer camp. Daphne shook her head, not so much to answer the question but to shake some sense into place. The tension started to fall away, and things came back into focus.

Daphne managed a small smile and yelled back, "It's me. I'm fine."

"You don't look so fine, Daphne, ten and a half," the woman responded with a concerned look on her face. "Can I give you a ride?"

Daphne glanced around with apprehension. She was lost and wet, but she knew better than to take rides from strangers.

"No, I just live over there," she replied, pointing up the street.

The woman must have sensed Daphne's concern because she rolled the window down even more, showing an empty passenger seat and camera equipment piled in the back.

"I was leaving the camp when I saw you walking. Then the rain came down, and I was worried. I started driving to find you, but you disappeared like a ghost. This was the first place I came to, so I thought I would drive through and make sure you made it okay. The storm is bad."

Daphne felt a sense of relief and told the woman about the cut-through, how she isn't really supposed to use it, and how she had gotten turned around.

"I see, I suppose you are probably in a bit of trouble then," the woman replied with a small laugh. "My name is Nila Lenski, and you are Daphne ten and a half, so now we are not strangers. Why don't you at least let me give you a ride to your street? You look less like my photogenic model and more like a wet mouse. I don't want you getting washed away with sewage."

The woman pointed to the storm drain near Daphne's feet. Daphne thought about it for a second. It would be nice to get out of the rain, and if she was dropped at the end of the street, Shane would never know. They weren't even strangers anymore, after all.

Daphne shrugged and made her way to the van. Nila reached over and opened the door for her. Daphne climbed into the van, stopping to clap her shoes together to get most of the mud off so as not to dirty the floor mat.

Nila looked at Daphne's shoes, a furrow between her brows, and said, "New cheer shoes, huh?"

Daphne looked down at them, taking in the damage now that she was out of the rain. "Yep, I think they are ruined. Mom is going to be mad for sure!"

Nila gave them a good look over and said, "They are scuffed, but I have something at my studio that will get them looking good as new. A few tricks of the trade."

Daphne looked up at Nila, hope in her eyes, and asked, "Really? You can get them looking new again? I thought they were ruined for sure."

Nila bobbed her head up and down a few times, then looked Daphne over, taking a moment to study her face.

"You know, even as a wet mouse, you have a lot of potential. Have you ever had headshots taken? You know, professionally, like models have?"

Daphne's eyes grew wide, "Professional pictures? Of me? No way!"

Nila looked at her as if this was a standard thing for every girl of ten and a half, a bit of surprise running across her features.

"Yes, you. You have beautiful eyes, shiny hair, and a pretty smile when you want to."

Daphne just looked at her speechless.

"I could take them for you. I have time today while I upload the pictures from today. I have things at my studio to clean you up. It wouldn't take much time."

Daphne wore a huge grin, spreading from ear to ear, then a thought crossed her mind and the smile faded.

"My parents are at work, and my brother isn't old enough to drive. Besides, I know I am going to be grounded forever for walking home alone. They will never pay for something like that now."

The disappointment hung on every syllable as Daphne spoke. Nila looked just as disappointed, almost heartbroken for the young girl.

"Well, I could take you now. I would do it for free. I could clean up those shoes while you freshen up, and then your parents can pick you up. You can tell them I kept you after to talk about it, so then no one must know about your secret hiking adventure." Nila was half laughing and half bouncing with excitement.

"Really, would you do that? But I don't have a way to call them, you know, to ask."

Nila reached into her pocket and pulled out a phone. "No worries, my little mouse. Give me a number, and I will call and explain everything. Us girls must stick together after all."

Daphne rattled off her mother's number as Nila punched the buttons. Her heartbeat faster as she listened to Nila explain what they had talked about, throwing in how the storm had come from nowhere and she had insisted Daphne wait inside with her. Daphne was practically wiggling in her seat when she heard Nila rattle off an address downtown and a time that she should be done.

Nila ended the call and turned to Daphne, "Well, my little mouse, are you ready to be a star?"

Daphne could hardly believe how her luck had changed. A few minutes ago, her world was crashing in on her, convinced she would never see the light of day again after the stunt she pulled. She made a mental note to stop watching those after-school specials as she fastened her seatbelt. She was going to be a model!

Nila glanced at the young girl as she put on her seatbelt. She could feel the excitement flowing out of her. Nila was just as excited. They were going to have so much fun, and the pictures were going to be a fantastic addition to her portfolio. Nila couldn't believe her luck! When she had lost the girl leaving the Y, she was sure she had failed. But now they were on their way. Nila was positive after the phone call that things were looking up. After all, she knew she had pleased him.

| 6 |

CHAPTER 6

CRANE, JANUARY 2022

It had been nearly a week since the tip first was viewed, and three weeks since it entered the queue. Crane's anger still burned, fueled by the regional office's failure to flag the file. How could they be so negligent? In a city teeming with a population of 316,000, not to mention the constant influx of tourists, the department had a mere two dedicated ICAC detectives and one Corporal. It was only thanks to grant money that funded their training and equipment that these detectives even existed. But two detectives were simply insufficient to handle the deluge of tips flooding in each month. The regional office was supposed to prioritize files involving potential live victims - victims desperately in need of rescue. As the detectives sifted through the endless sea of tips, these victims silently prayed for their knight in shining armor to save them from their harrowing circumstances. Meanwhile, miles away from headquarters, children were enduring unimaginable abuse, while the detectives sat behind their computers, typing, and clicking away.

This particular file hadn't been given any indication of priority, which meant others had been placed ahead of it. By the time Crane and Adams reached this tip on their never-ending list, eleven days had slipped away. At first glance, it seemed to be just photographs of a young girl asleep, with an unknown man engaged in explicit acts, capturing it all on a phone camera. Then, additional images surfaced of an adult woman also in slumber. Two days after the initial tip, another message arrived, this time containing videos of the same girl, appearing to be asleep, the same male stroking her hair with one hand and his genitals with the other. More images of the young girl enduring the same horrifying acts, but now they had a visual of the abuser. It was Adams who first noticed the familiar background in one of the videos, matching that of one of the photographs featuring the adult woman. They were all connected. The man, the woman, and the child. And now, with an IP address in their possession, they had a lead to follow.

They took their findings to Corporal Vickers, beginning the arduous process of obtaining warrants from various service providers. Once they had an address and the woman's name, they delved into the depths of social media, where they discovered the family. They had a live victim in their city, suffering a mere seven miles away. Working in tandem, Crane and Adams tirelessly worked to secure a search warrant for the suspect's home and phone. Within two days, they accomplished their goal, rallying the support of the Special Victims Unit and the Fugitive Investigation Unit just two days later.

Now, they found themselves in the midst of a search within the confines of a tiny home, scouring every nook and cranny for any trace of electronics, electronic storage devices, photographs, or DVDs that could potentially contain evidence of child sexual abuse materials. The suspect had almost made his escape when the fugitive unit swiftly apprehended him. With the home now cleared, the detectives were given the green light to commence their investigation.

This cramped dwelling consisted of just one bedroom and one bathroom. Interestingly, what appeared to be a dining room had been transformed into a small space dedicated to a child. The entire home couldn't have exceeded more than seven hundred square feet. Not too long ago, a mother and daughter had rented this place. Curiously, an old twin mattress leaned against the kitchen wall near the back door. The entire home resembled nothing more than a haphazard pile of belongings stacked upon one another. Upon closer inspection of the photographs, Crane confirmed this was indeed the correct location.

After two hours of thorough searching, they had already documented a page and a half of evidence. Within the first fifteen minutes, they stumbled upon a small tablet, prompting the digital forensic team to spring into action. Their goal was to find ten incriminating photographs, videos, or a combination of both. Astonishingly, the team achieved this feat in less than thirty minutes. Crane, feeling a bit unsettled, stepped outside the back door to catch some fresh air, hoping it would help ground her. There, just a few feet away, sat their suspect in handcuffs. Known as Angel Figueroa-Rodriguez, a twenty-eight-year-old with no apparent job or criminal record, his connection to the child and mother remained a mystery.

Initially, Angel had been quite talkative upon their arrival, but since then, he had fallen into an eerie silence. He had yet to request a lawyer, and technically, he wasn't under arrest until Adams finished drafting the arrest warrant, which couldn't begin until the digital team completed their tasks. As the patrol officers took over the evidence collection, Adams sat in the car, diligently working on the arrest warrant. Vickers, on the other hand, engaged in a phone conversation with the mother. Meanwhile, Crane kept a watchful eye on Angel. Soon, he would be transported to headquarters for a formal interview, making this observation period crucial. Every word he uttered, his reactions to the conversations around him, and his responses to the items being removed from the home were all vital pieces of information. It was imperative to minimize direct interaction, asking only the most essential questions, and not revealing his arrest status until the warrant was signed. The last thing they needed was for him to assert his rights prematurely, before they had gathered enough evidence for an arrest or conducted the interview.

Television dramas always depict police officers storming in with guns drawn, kicking down doors, and swiftly apprehending suspects while reciting the Miranda rights. In the background, a young officer holding up a single folded paper while shouting, "search warrant!" But that's not how it unfolds in reality. The truth is, the process of obtaining a search warrant is time-consuming and often involves the SWAT team, although in some cases, like today, they aren't required. First, the occupants of the premises are identified and the house is secured, either through a knock on the door or by surprise, just as it happened with Angel today. Then, the officers meticulously read the warrant word by word before commencing the search. Contrary to popular belief, not all search warrants result in arrests, and not everyone who is handcuffed needs to be informed of their rights, even if they end up being taken into custody.

However, Angel will be read Miranda rights, as each officer carries a small card for that purpose. This ensures that when they are called to testify, they can assert with certainty that the suspect was properly informed of their rights. Miranda only applies if the intention is to question the suspect while in custody. In many cases, law enforcement already has enough evidence to make an arrest without uttering a single word.

Therefore, Crane merely observes, carefully noting every detail of Angel's demeanor - every nod, fidget, twitch, blink, and sigh. Crane is preparing for the upcoming interview and strategizing on how to approach it. Although they already have sufficient evidence for an arrest, in cases like this, it's crucial to gather as much information as possible. Given that the victim is so young, her testimony may not hold significant weight on its own, necessitating additional evidence. Crane isn't just interested in the motive behind the crime; Crane desires a comprehensive understanding of the entire world that exists beyond the pristine picket fences, flawlessly manicured lawns, and festive holiday decorations. Crane wants to uncover the depths of the people who hunger for these disturbing videos and pictures, the individuals who trade children as if they were mere baseball cards.

***

Crane found herself in the small viewing room, surrounded by two desks and a multitude of screens. Each screen provided a different perspective into an interview room. Gone were the days of hidden rooms behind two-way mirrors. This space was sleek and modern, equipped with keycard access readers and doors that automatically locked upon closure. The rooms were soundproof and outfitted with two cameras, capturing both the back and front of the area. From the comfort of the viewing room, an officer could observe interviews or suspects while simultaneously working on their reports or charging affidavits. And it was here that Crane sat, attentively watching Angel, who appeared to be deep in slumber. She decided to give him a few moments before diving into the interview.

Just then, Adams entered, breaking Crane's train of thought.

"Giving him time to freeze up, huh?" he quipped.

It was a technique they often employed - letting the suspects feel the chill in the air, uncertainty creeping in, before swooping in with a warm blanket and some water. Their approach remained calm and sympathetic, apologizing for the wait and assuring a swift process so they could "get back on their way." Unfamiliar individuals might interpret this as a sign that a simple conversation could clear up any misunderstandings and allow them to return home. However, those who had encountered the system before knew better. They understood that this was just the beginning of their journey towards incarceration. With such individuals, Crane and Adams had to adapt their strategy, either adopting a nonchalant attitude or resorting to tough love - anything to prevent that dreaded word from escaping their mouths: "lawyer."

"Yeah, I had higher hopes for the mother's cooperation," Crane lamented, shaking her head with a heavy sigh. "How does someone defend a person after being told he drugged them and their child, engaging in God knows what?"

It baffled her. Angel turned out to be the mother's cousin, seeking refuge with them after her divorce. She claimed he was only "helping" with her daughter and would never harm her. The excuses poured forth, just as they always did. However, Crane couldn't help but feel disappointed. Adams took a seat beside her, his expression mirroring her disgust.

"She even refused to bring her daughter to victim services," he disclosed. "We had to contact the ex-husband, who picked the child up from school. Thankfully, the victim center is scheduled to interview the little girl tomorrow. Vickers made the call to DCF; maybe they can assist the father in obtaining temporary custody while we sort through this mess. It's appalling how the mother didn't even flinch when we informed her about the explicit photos Angel took of her and her daughter."

Crane's stomach twisted in knots, threatening to betray her composure.

The question hung in the air like a heavy cloud: "Do we know how long Angel has been staying there?"

She dreaded the answer, knowing it would only worsen her already sinking feeling. Adams seemed to read her mind, fixating his gaze on the screen before responding.

"There was no way we could have known, you know that. Once we had the lead, we acted swiftly. Don't blame yourself. Based on our estimates, he moved in about six months ago, but he's had access to her since birth."

Crane's voice barely escaped as a whisper, "Do you truly believe that?

They found new videos. That little girl was just seven miles away, and we couldn't save her." Adams, a father of two girls, absentmindedly twisted his wedding ring. No words were needed; Crane knew he shared her anguish.

They sat in silence, fixated on the screen, each consumed by thoughts of two innocent little girls. Adams couldn't help but picture his own daughters, his precious princesses, their smiling faces adorning his office walls. Crane's mind traveled to two other little girls, one frozen in time at age ten, the other at eleven, their futures reduced to mere speculations as Crane tirelessly searched for answers.

Crane cleared her throat, stretching her tired muscles before gathering her notepad and small recorder. Casting one last glance at the monitor, she gently squeezed Adams' shoulder.

"I suppose he's been kept on ice long enough."

Crane walked out of the room, grabbing a blanket and soda she had left outside the interview room door. She smoothed her clothes and took a deep breath before swiping her access card.

From the viewing room, Adams watched intently as Crane entered the interview room. Angel's head lifted off the table, startled by her presence. He observed his partner shifting the handcuffs from the back to the front, carefully draping a blanket over Angel's shoulders, making sure it was snug. Crane opened the can of soda and placed it in front of Angel, sitting down and moving her chair closer. Her demeanor transformed, light and comforting, as if Angel was a dear friend in need of solace. In those moments, Adams couldn't help but envy Crane's ability to compartmentalize her pain and emotions. He envied her freedom from witnessing this darkness and then having to go home and tell two little princesses what a wonderful place the world was.

| 7 |

CHAPTER 7

VANESSA, DECEMBER 2009

From the minute Vanessa walked into the studio, she vowed that no one was going to ruin her day. Yes, today was about her. She was finally going to be a star. It didn't matter to Vanessa how she got the lead part; it only mattered that she was the lead, she was the Sugar Plum Fairy. Vanessa had ignored Abigail during the short ride to the studio. Abby's words had done their job; they had stung and thrown Vanessa's confidence for a whirl. Vanessa had stewed until she felt the negativity engulfing her. She couldn't afford anything but the glow of perfection today, so she pushed it down, shook it off, and even managed a smile as she jumped out of the car, giving her sister a half wave as she ran to the door.

When the glass doors closed behind her, so did all the memories of that morning. Vanessa threw her small shoulders back, squared her chin, making herself as tall and graceful as she possibly could. This was it, this was her day, her time to prove she had what it took.

Almost immediately, the other girls swarmed around Vanessa, talking at her, not necessarily to her, as if she held all the answers. Vanessa felt the buzzing energy start to make its way into her body, under her skin. She felt energized and confident, ready to take on any task. Even with all the attention, she was anxious to put on the Sugar Plum Fairy costume. She had dreamt about it all night. It was the most beautiful outfit Vanessa had ever seen, and her skin ached to be wrapped in it.

Out of nowhere, she heard Mrs. Blanchard's voice, "Vanessa, are you here? Where are you, dear?"

Vanessa looked over the crowd of tightly fixed buns until she spotted her Ballet Master. Mrs. Blanchard was exactly what one would expect from a small-town Ballet Studio owner. She was tall and lean, with dark hair streaked with gray, the only real evidence of her true age. Mrs. Blanchard had been a ballerina with the Bolshoi Ballet. Vanessa did not know much about that, but she knew it was a famous company and that Mrs. Blanchard had been wonderful. There weren't many photographs of her as a young ballerina, just those of her with her students. However, once, Vanessa had seen Mrs. Blanchard staring at an old photograph of a beautiful girl in the most graceful pose. It looked like an old poster with writing she didn't recognize.

When Vanessa had asked her about it, Mrs. Blanchard had a tear in her eye and simply said, "That is me, when dance was all I knew, before I understood the world." Then Mrs. Blanchard had put the photograph away, and they never spoke of it again.

"Over here, Madame Blanchard," Vanessa announced over the group of giggles and excitement.

"Come, girl, we have much to do. You need to dress; the photography team should be here any minute. You want to look your best, yes?"

With that, Vanessa made her way through the group, who began to disperse and gather at the bars to stretch. She followed Mrs. Blanchard into the dressing area. As she entered the room, she saw it—the beautiful costume hanging in the middle of the room, standing out from the others. The bright white chiffon, the color of snow, the light pink silk, and the gold trims all seemed to glow under the warm light. There were matching white tights, white ballet shoes, and a small tiara. Vanessa couldn't take her eyes off the outfit. It was more glorious than she had dreamt. She had seen it before when Lisa had her fittings, but now she would be wearing it.

Mrs. Blanchard was rushing about the small space, moving things, picking up things, and muttering under her breath. Vanessa snapped back to the studio and the task at hand. She dropped her small duffle bag in a corner and began taking off her shoes and jacket. Mrs. Blanchard moved over to the costume and started to unhang it, laying it out in pieces.

"Come, child. We haven't any time to waste. I'll leave you to it and check on the photographer," Mrs. Blanchard said.

Vanessa felt a quick burst of air as the door shut to give her privacy to change.

Vanessa took her time with the stockings, careful not to tear them. She added the layers piece by piece, handling each one as if it were made of glass and could shatter at the slightest movement. Minute by minute, she was transforming from a smart-mouthed eleven-year-old child into an elegant figurine that you might see on a shelf at one of those fancy stores. Vanessa was beginning to feel herself changing inside with each added piece. She felt lighter, taller, and more graceful. Vanessa stared at the transformation in the small mirror in the corner, the tiara in hand. Visions of her future dancing in Paris, New York, England, Prague danced through her mind.

Vanessa was so involved in her thoughts that she hadn't even noticed the door open or the woman watching her. The woman stood very still as she took in every detail of the girl in front of her. The girl was tall and lean, her hair dark like chestnuts, pulled into a tight bun on the top of her head. Her shoulders were squared back, her neck long, and her chin high. She moved with elegance and grace, far beyond that of a girl her age. The woman watched, lost in reflection before her. The woman thought it would be easy to get a perfect shot of her for the brochure. In her head, she was already picturing poses, angles, and lighting. It had been a while since the woman had been this excited for a shoot.

Just then, the door swung open farther, making way for Mrs. Blanchard and a swarm of other small girls. If the girl in the mirror had been startled, the woman saw no sign of it. She almost dropped her camera with the sudden change of energy in the room.

"I see you found each other," the older lady said to the woman, barely giving her a look.

"Sort of, I just got here. We haven't been introduced," the woman said.

"Well, let's get to it. Vanessa, are you ready? This is the photographer who is going to take your picture. You will use the small studio. I imagine you are all set up?" she said, now addressing the woman.

The woman gave a nod of her head, indicating she was ready to begin, and Vanessa turned, looking at her for the first time. Yes, she was going to take a lovely photograph indeed.

***

A short time later, the woman and Vanessa began their shoot in the small studio off the main studio. The young girl posed gracefully and took direction extremely well. However, the woman was sure she could capture a better picture. She scrolled through the pictures she had taken with a look of frustration. The girl must have picked up on it because she suddenly looked over the woman's shoulder.

"That is me? I can hardly tell!"

Vanessa was amazed by the pictures. She knew they were of her, but she felt like she was looking at someone else. Like some other beautiful creature, something not even real.

"Of course, it is you, silly goose," the woman giggled and started looking back through the photographs. "You take amazing pictures, but I feel I can capture something even more spectacular. I'm just not sure what I am missing," the woman said, mostly speaking to herself.

"I can try some other poses. Maybe something a bit harder?"

"I don't think that is it. You look graceful in all these shots," the woman stared at the picture for a few more seconds. "Your makeup, we need to do something with your makeup."

"I tried to get my sister to help me this morning, but she doesn't like to do anything to help me. She always says I am a hindrance to her social life. Whatever that means."

The woman laughed a little, trying to hide her smile. "I know exactly what you mean. I can help; I always bring things with me. I used to practice on my cousins when I was little, I loved doing their hair and makeup."

"Wow, I wish you could be my sister then. The only thing Abby likes to do with me is trade insults."

The woman had already begun to lay out some different palettes and lipsticks. There were so many different colors and brushes, more than Vanessa had ever seen. The woman indicated for Vanessa to sit in front of her as she started looking from Vanessa to the palettes and back to Vanessa. It only took a few minutes and a couple of swipes over her cheeks, then her eyes, and lastly her lips. Vanessa asked if she could see herself in the small mirror, but the woman had said for her to go back under the lights and imagine herself as the most beautiful ballerina she had ever seen. Vanessa remembered the picture Mrs.

Blanchard had held that day, and she imagined herself looking that way on a poster.

A few clicks and instructions from the woman, then a few more clicks, and they were finally finished. The woman called Vanessa over and first showed her the original pictures they had taken. Then she swiped to the last five pictures, showing Vanessa the photos she had just taken. Vanessa's breath was taken away. She looked perfect. The makeup was stunning. Not too much, but enough to make her cheeks sharper, her lips plumper, and her eyes bigger. Vanessa couldn't believe that was her, that she was looking at herself.

"Not too bad, huh?" The woman was smiling from ear to ear. She seemed as excited, if not more, than Vanessa.

"Not bad? They are perfect! I can't believe everyone is going to see me looking like this on the brochure. My sister is going to die!"

The woman was thrilled with her work and even happier with the change in the girl's confidence. The woman loved bringing the beauty she saw to life through her lens. It was one of the few joys she had in life. It was moments like these that made her love her job, love being behind a camera.

"Have you ever had your picture taken before?" the woman asked.

"I mean, of course, we have family pictures done every year, and I have a Polaroid camera that I love to take pictures with. My mom says that when I am older, she will get me a real camera. She just wants to make sure I am responsible enough because she says they are expensive. I want to learn to develop my own pictures too."

The woman could see the light in Vanessa's eyes when she talked about photography. It wasn't anything near the light she had when she posed as a ballerina, but it was there.

"No, I mean like today. Just of you. Like for modeling or something. You have the look and talent for it."

The woman tried not to let her excitement overtake her as she spoke, but it was difficult after seeing the images she had just created.

"I've never done that. My sister is the pretty one. No one has ever wanted to take my picture, except for school or dance," Vanessa replied shyly.

"Well, I would love to make you a portfolio! You will need it as you go further with your dancing, and it will help me get exposure as a photographer in the area. I could do it for free, for the practice, but you just have to tell people it was my studio who took them. I can give you my card, and you can set something up with your parents." The woman waited in anticipation for Vanessa's answer.

"I'm sort of in trouble right now, and I have the show in two days. My sister would have to bring me, and she won't be doing me any favors anytime soon."

Vanessa couldn't hide the disappointment in her voice, and it broke the woman's heart. Vanessa thanked the woman who had begun to pack up, then rushed off to the dressing room to change.

***

Vanessa had returned all the pieces where she found them, taking in the costume one last time before heading to the front of the studio. Mrs. Blanchard had already printed off a rough copy of the brochure and handed it to Vanessa. They were both wearing huge smiles.

Vanessa looked at Mrs. Blanchard and said, "I imagined I was you, like in that old picture you have for this picture. That is why it is so perfect."

Vanessa hugged Mrs. Blanchard and walked out the front doors toward a row of benches where she sat to wait for Abby. Mrs. Blanchard was overcome with emotion, rushing to the safety of her office. Once there, she let the flood of tears start rolling down her cheeks as the hum of the printer covered her sobs.

As Vanessa sat waiting, she couldn't stop looking at the brochure. She felt like she was staring at a stranger. She let herself imagine being on stage, performing with some of the great Prima Ballerinas. The audience applauded louder and louder. At some point, the applause took on the sound of a car horn, jolting Vanessa back to reality. Vanessa started to get up, expecting to see Abby impatiently waiting at the curb with that annoyed look on her face.

Instead, Vanessa saw a familiar face waving to her from an unfamiliar blue SUV.

"Hey Vanessa, you're still here. Is everything okay?"

Vanessa got up and walked closer to the vehicle so she wouldn't have to shout.

"I'm good, just waiting on my sister. She's always late." Vanessa gave the last statement emphasis by rolling her eyes.

The woman smiled and said, "I was thinking, I have the rest of the afternoon free, and I'm sure it would score some major points with your sister. I can take you to my studio around the corner and work on that portfolio, then you can have someone pick you up there in a few hours. It's just a few minutes from here, so it isn't out of the way. It could give your sister extra time to work on that social life," the woman added with a laugh.

Vanessa laughed with her, then explained she didn't have a phone, but she could probably use Mrs. Blanchard's phone to call. Vanessa said she still wasn't sure if her mom would be okay with it since she was still in trouble for this morning.

The woman said it wasn't a big deal; she could call Vanessa's mom from her phone and tell her that they hadn't gotten a good picture for the brochure. She could tell her she had a better scenery at her studio and could give Vanessa a ride if someone could pick her up in an hour or so. The woman said she was sure it would be okay since Mrs. Blanchard had hired her, and Vanessa's mom knew Mrs. Blanchard.

Vanessa began to feel excited all over again. This was going to be her day. Vanessa hopped in the passenger seat and recited her mother's number by heart. She felt anxiety running through her veins as the woman pushed the numbers on her cellphone. She closed her eyes and crossed her fingers as the woman spoke into the phone.

"Hi, is this Mrs. Crane? This is Nila Lenski. I am the photographer Mrs. Blanchard hired for the brochure......."

The rest of the conversation was a blur, and Vanessa hadn't realized she had been holding her breath until she heard Nila say, "It's no problem at all. Yes, an hour or so should be plenty. Do you need the address again? Okay, great. I will see you later."

Nila hung up the phone and turned to Vanessa, "Put on your seatbelt, my dancing queen. We have pictures to take!"

Vanessa let out a deep breath. She felt dizzy with excitement. Every inch of her body was vibrating with energy. She said today was going to be about her, that it was going to be her day. A day to remember, and it was!

Nila could feel the energy exuding from Vanessa. This was going to be an epic photoshoot. There was something special about this girl; she could feel it in her bones. Nila could hold on to the pure joy of the moment if she only thought about today. The rest was for another time. She was going to feel this happiness for a while. She earned it; she had pleased him.

| 8 |

CHAPTER 8

HARRIS, JANUARY 2022

As the wheels rolled on, Harris couldn't help but question how he had allowed himself to be talked into embarking on this adventure. It had been over two thrilling weeks in Thailand, yet restlessness had started to seep into the group. The grueling training sessions were balanced by the merciful weather, making the outdoor activities surprisingly enjoyable. However, the team had unanimously decided to let loose this weekend, ready to shed their disciplined facade.

Their accommodations, while contemporary and comfortable, were situated just outside the bustling city, tucked away in a secluded spot. This was the usual arrangement whenever they traveled. The team, preferring the intimacy of temporary rentals over impersonal hotels, always sought out peaceful, off-the-beaten-path locations. It afforded them a cloak of anonymity, allowing them to come and go unnoticed, while minimizing any security concerns due to the lack of prying eyes. Each morning, they would load into the nondescript van, heading towards the training facility. Sharing the responsibility, they took turns cooking hearty breakfasts, while relishing the opportunity to dine with the esteemed Royal Thai Military for lunch. As night fell, they would either whip up a delicious meal together, stop by a local eatery before leaving the city, or simply grab a quick bite from one of the charming establishments near their cottage.

They flatly rejected any of the concierge services offered by the company managing the property. They preferred minimal foot traffic in and out. The reservation was cleverly made under a false holding company, and the men disguised themselves as businessmen. Their true identities were known only to the select eight members of their team, and their purpose here was only revealed to those involved in the joint military training exercise. Anonymity was paramount, whether they were training with friendly nations off American soil or traveling within the United States.

Each team member had a crucial role to fulfill, contributing to the mission's success. Moreover, they formed a tight-knit family structure where their lives depended on one another. Among them, Harris assumed the role of the big brother. Although not the highest-ranking or most senior, he commanded respect due to his experience and wisdom. Harris possessed a unique ability to diffuse tense situations, radiating a sense of calm that compelled the others to listen intently to his words.

The journey from Nong Mai Daen in Northern Chon Buri to Pattaya City in Southern Chon Buri lasted just over an hour. Usually, Harris would have stayed behind, but this time he decided to take the wheel. He wasn't much of a drinker or a partygoer, so he volunteered to drive and keep an eye on the four others who were eager to make the trip.

The two newest members of the team, Buck and Ace, had been chatting incessantly since they set off. Slim, who was unlucky enough to be stuck in the backseat with them, couldn't resist joining the conversation as the excitement of the night grew closer. Up front, Harris had Pop as his companion. Amongst the guys, Harris had earned the nickname "Doc" due to his eloquence with words the guys coined as his bedside manner and preference for books over people. Pop, the most senior member and highest-ranking, was the glue that held them all together. While Harris used verbal judo to defuse tense situations, Pop had the power to do the same with just a single glance.

Harris was surprised that Pop had decided to come along, but he suspected it was more about working through his second divorce than the allure of nightlife. Meanwhile, Hawk and Phantom had stayed behind, engrossed in an intense and ongoing game of chess at a small table in the den. Harris couldn't help but envy them as he listened to Buck and Ace eagerly discuss getting drunk and finding casual encounters.

Unlike them, Harris had no interest in either. He never quite saw the appeal of fleeting encounters with unfamiliar faces in the darkness. He had experienced his fair share of romantic encounters but always sought something more meaningful than a nameless stranger. Having been to Thailand before, Harris knew that the trip to Pattaya and its famous walking street was considered a rite of passage for the guys.

Harris wasn't exactly a stick in the mud, but the glitz and glamour of the city didn't appeal to him. He preferred a more focused and purposeful life, always striving for the next adventure or opportunity to break free from the constraints that held him back. The flashing lights, booming music, scantily clad women, and drugs being passed around like candy simply weren't his scene. He valued being in control of his mind and actions, ready to face any situation that came his way.

As they approached the strip, Harris directed his steps towards Bali Hai, where they could find public parking. Meanwhile, Pop began his customary briefing to the group.

"Keep your heads on a swivel, don't wander off alone, wrap it before you tap it, don't add or subtract from the population, and if you find yourself in trouble, I have no fucking clue who you assholes are."

Pop's words were familiar, and yet everyone knew he would be the first to come to their aid if needed.

The newer members of the group looked ahead wide-eyed, as if bracing themselves for a culture shock. Harris almost let out a chuckle, realizing they were about to experience something completely out of their comfort zones.

With their instructions in hand and the vehicle secured, the five amigos embarked on their journey toward the bustling strip opening. As darkness blanketed the road, it became off-limits to vehicles, policed by local authorities stationed at both ends. The night air throbbed with a cacophony of conflicting melodies emanating from various establishments, enveloping the amigos in a symphony of sound. Neon signs illuminated the path, beckoning with promises of delectable seafood, live music, pulsating discotheques, mesmerizing go-go bars, and thrilling Muay Thai matches. The streets teemed with a vibrant blend of locals and tourists, creating an electric atmosphere.

Amongst the crowd, Harris observed a flurry of activity as guys attempted to capture the attention of the girls promoting the different clubs through their camera lenses. Such behavior was frowned upon, and Harris was well aware of it. He watched as the alluringly dressed girls, donning outfits ranging from schoolgirls to maids and cheerleaders, skillfully evaded the cameras. If the patrons persisted, the girls would retreat inside while bouncers took their place, gently persuading the amateur photographers to move along. The girls were rotated every half hour, ensuring a constant stream of fresh faces on the lively street. Some venues even offered glimpses through windows of dancing women, providing a tantalizing preview of the performances awaiting behind a modest cover charge.

The vibrant streets were bustling with local vendors offering a plethora of handmade crafts and beautiful flowers. Amidst the lively atmosphere, there were the daring promoters who would approach men with an intriguing proposition - a selection of enticing sex shows. They would present a meticulously designed menu laden with captivating photographs of sexualized women, allowing the patrons to choose like they would an appetizer at a fine restaurant. While the promoters promised a tantalizing peep-style performance by the woman of their choice, it was no secret that many of these women were professionals offering much more than just a show. For those who preferred a less audacious encounter, the bar girls within the venues were always an option. These captivating "women" were con-fined within the establishment's walls, forbidden from venturing out-side. However, for a modest "bar fine," a patron could be escorted away by one of these charismatic ladies.

To the intoxicated and lustful patrons who frequented the dazzling establishments clad with American monikers like "SkyFall" or "Alca-traz," this was all part of the thrilling game. It was the accepted norm, where questions about the origin of these women, their age, or even their safety were rarely raised. But Harris, having traveled to count-less places, couldn't help but ponder these very questions whenever he came across situations and circumstances like these. The thrill had long faded for him. Deep down, he knew that some of these women were not women at all, and he couldn't help but imagine their silent prayers for a savior who would never come.

***

As the clock struck midnight, Harris couldn't help but glance at his watch once again. Hours ago, Buck, Ace, and Slim had disappeared into one of the electrifying go-go clubs that decorated the bustling strip. Meanwhile, Harris and Pop had settled themselves in a lively sports bar, embracing the open-air seating it offered. Harris had de-voured his meal and downed two refreshing beers, while Pop had upgraded his brew to the potent Sang Som. Initially, Pop had been cautious with his alcohol intake, but now he teetered on the edge between a pleasant buzz and an outright drunken stupor. His eyes, glazed and unfocused, struggled to comprehend the exhilarating fight unfolding on the colossal TV screens. The raucous crowd surrounding them oscillated between hurling profanities and erupting into thunderous applause. They had all agreed to rendezvous at the strip's entrance by 0200.

Harris's eyes locked onto his watch once more, realizing that there was still a grueling hour and a half remaining before their designated meeting time, followed by an arduous hour-long drive back. He couldn't shake off the gnawing feeling that Buck, Ace, and Slim were in a similar, if not worse, inebriated state as Pop. The prospect of navigating the winding roads with them was enough to send shivers down Harris's spine. Ignoring any semblance of consent, Pop called for another round of drinks, his attention firmly fixated on the local rivalry playing out on the television screen. Harris was convinced that Pop, caught up in the fervor of the moment, was mindlessly joining the chorus of cheers and jeers. However, after the somber conversation they had shared earlier, delving into the depths of Pop's youngest son's struggles and the heart-wrenching divorce, Harris found solace in witnessing Pop's newfound tranquility.

Harris motioned to Pop, signaling his need for a breath of fresh air and set off on a leisurely stroll. He knew that the pier at the far end of the bustling strip would offer solace during this late hour. The majority of tourists, satiated by music and cuisine, would have departed on gondolas or ferries to their respective resorts. Harris nonchalantly tossed a handful of baht, the local currency, on the table, more than enough to settle their bill and also cover a few extra drinks. He planned to return shortly to fetch Pop before heading to the designated meeting spot for the rest of the group.

The placid ambiance and the gentle breeze from the water would revitalize Harris before he took on the onerous task of transporting the inebriated men to the van for the hour-long journey back to their cottage. It wasn't that Harris didn't appreciate a night out or indulging in a drink, but he had his fair share of revelry during his younger years. In high school, he would occasionally venture to the ball field with a case of beer supplied by older kids, seeking solace and temporary respite from the memories that haunted him. Baseball had once consumed his entire existence, his dreams encompassing collegiate play, followed by a stint in the minor leagues, and ultimately a shot at the pros.

As he returned to the field that had consumed his youth, a symphony of familiar sounds enveloped him. The chatter of his teammates echoed from the dugout, the coach's voice boomed as he called out drills, and the resounding crack of the bat meeting a blazing fastball reverberated through the air. There were even moments when he could catch a whiff of the oil from his trusty glove and the intoxicating blend of sweat and freshly cut grass clinging to his uniform. But like all childhood dreams, this one faded with the passage of time, not in years counted by birthdays, but in the profound moments that shape one's life.

One fateful summer, a lightning bolt of change struck Harris' family, and in a matter of days, he aged a decade. He never stepped foot on the baseball field again after that season, but he found solace in the late-night visits to the sacred ground. There, he could still hear the echoes of the game, the sounds and smells that only reached out to him, and he would drown his sorrows in the silence that followed.

As Harris ventured past the brightly lit signs and towering windows, he noticed a peculiar noise that stood out amidst the bustling atmosphere. Despite the few people lingering in this corner of the strip, it was far from quiet. Every sound around him carried a distinct identity. The shuffle of feet as equipment was moved, the gentle rustle of cardboard as boxes were carefully packed and stacked, the soft melodies drifting from the rear doors as workers took a momentary break, and even the metallic clang of trash being discarded into bins.

The lighting, although dim, seemed fitting for the setting, as if it were a natural conclusion to the night's events.

Harris adjusted his pace, his eyes fixed ahead as he absorbed every detail of his surroundings. Suddenly, the noise came again, slightly louder this time - a thud, followed by shuffling and an indistinct sound in the distance. Two people, that much was clear from the different types of shoe scuffs. The thud didn't resemble a fall, yet it wasn't loud enough to be something discarded. As Harris continued towards the pier, he felt certain that the source of the sounds was to his right, just ahead. He contemplated turning back, the thought of encountering something unexpected as a lone tourist in the middle of the night unnerving him. The last thing he wanted was to draw attention to himself, especially in this unfamiliar place.

Just as Harris was on the brink of retracing his steps, he identified the faint noise once again, now slightly louder. It was a whimper, muffled and filled with sorrow. Accompanying it was a deeper, slurred voice engaging in a one-sided conversation. Although Harris couldn't decipher any words, the tone conveyed a sense of urgency and distress. He moved closer to the row of buildings on his right, carefully navigating through the shadows. Just about ten feet ahead, he noticed a narrow opening where one of the spaces was undergoing renovation. The board covering the door had been removed, suggesting recent activity. However, there were no signs of light or any indication that work was being done in the area. The dim lighting provided some concealment, but it hindered his ability to see inside.

Harris cautiously approached the entrance, his senses heightened, scanning for any signs of unusual activity or lurking figures in the shadows. Although he felt confident that he was alone outside, he couldn't shake the certainty that the source of the strange noises originated from within. As Harris peered through the dim lighting, he caught a glimpse of a shadowy figure—a man who appeared stockier and shorter than him. The words being exchanged were incomprehensible, muffled by slurred speech and stifled sobs. Yet, Harris was convinced that it was a broken form of English, or perhaps an attempt at it. Initially, he speculated that it could have been a lovers' disagreement, an affair he had no business meddling in. His best course of action was to retreat before drawing any attention.

Suddenly, a piercing cry shattered the air, followed by the unmistakable sound of a forceful slap across someone's face. The man bellowed two words, one of which Harris suspected might be Russian. In broken English, the girl pleaded desperately for the man to cease his actions. It was evident that she was Thai. A chill raced down Harris' spine, dispelling any notion of a mere lovers' spat. Deep down, he knew that this situation was far from his concern. Outside of his training, he had no place interfering. Harris anxiously scanned his surroundings, hoping to catch sight of a patrolling member of the Thai Police. The strip wasn't officially closed until 0400, so they should still be active.

Harris found himself in a situation that sent chills down his spine. As he scanned the dimly lit room, he realized he was the only witness to something sinister. It was no mere coincidence; the man inside had deliberately chosen a hidden spot where he could carry out his wicked intentions undisturbed. Harris cautiously peered inside, his eyes adjusting to the darkness. The man's back was turned, but Harris could just make out a pair of trembling legs pressed against the wall. The man's heavy hand was planted dangerously close to the girl's head, while the other hand remained concealed from view. Shifting his weight to one leg, the man inadvertently revealed a chilling sight. The girl, much younger than her assailant, bore a battered face, her body convulsing with each sob. It became clear to Harris what was happening when the man's hand descended from the wall.

The man's grip tightened around the girl's delicate neck, her bar uniform torn and her fear palpable. This was no ordinary encounter; this girl was not a professional, but a terrified victim. The man's anger radiated from him, and Harris knew he had mere seconds to devise a plan. He desperately searched for any advantage, but the world beyond offered no assistance. Everything he needed was on the other side of that entrance, but he had no clue who or what awaited him there. The absence of a visible weapon didn't guarantee the man's lack of weapons or accomplices. As the man's pants sagged from his waist, the girl's sobs grew louder, echoing their urgency. Harris knew that the time to act was now or never.

With his best southern twang, Harris unleashed a soulful rendition of "ALLLLLLLLLL my exxxeees lives in Texezzz." He stumbled a bit, struggling to find his footing as he navigated through a maze of apps on his phone. The soft glow of the screen offered a glimpse of his immediate surroundings. As he took a few unsteady steps forward, Harris surveyed the open space, relieved to find himself alone and the tension lifting from his shoulders. Closing in on the couple, he belted out another line, "that's why I haaaaanggg my cap.."

Suddenly, the smaller man spun around, diverting his attention from the girl to Harris. His Russian-accented English slurred with anger, he barked, "What the fuck? Who da fuck are you?"

His bloodshot eyes darted around, searching for any signs of companionship.

Harris feigned surprise, his face morphing into an expression of innocence.

"Whoooa fella, pardon me ma'am. I didn't mee'an to disturb your... uh, what is it I'm disturbin'?"

With wide eyes, he let out a loud belch, then continued to scan the area, a look of bewilderment on his face. Returning to his phone, Harris absentmindedly rubbed his knuckles against his chin.

"I beg your par... pardon, I think I might be lost."

"Damn right you are lost, nothing here is for you. Get the fuck out of here before you ruin my buzz and my erection." The man looked Harris in the eyes, taking one half step, half sway in his direction. "You dumb American assholes, always trying to fuck up somebodies good time."

Harris shifted his gaze towards the young woman desperately clutching her torn dress, struggling to maintain her balance. Her left eye was already swollen, and a cut on her lip dripped blood down her chin onto her chest. Though she remained silent, her wide eyes betrayed her fear. From this distance, Harris estimated she couldn't be more than seventeen. He now noticed the healing scars on her wrists and fading bruises on her thighs.

"Well, I might be dumb alright, but it doesn't seem to me the little lady there is having much of a good time,"

Harris retorted, engaging in a tense staring match with the man. Though the man was older and shorter, Harris knew better than to underestimate him. It was an open secret that the Russian mob had deep connections within the Pattaya club scene. The girl probably worked at one of the clubs owned by a Russian corporation. The question remained whether this man was just an overly handsy tourist or a dangerous acquaintance. Regardless, it spelled trouble for the girl, who clearly wasn't willingly participating in tonight's "fun."

"What that girl is up to or not up to is none of your business. You can either disappear elsewhere or vanish for good."

The last part slipped out like a venomous whisper, revealing the man's fading bravado. Meanwhile, the girl remained motionless, seemingly unfazed by the commotion. Harris knew that if he abandoned her, she would likely disappear forever.

"Alright, alright, no need to get your knickers in a twist. I've never been one to be a third wheel. No harm done, buddy. If you just point me in the direction of this place, I'll be on my merry way."

Harris gestured at his phone, indicating that he had a specific destination in mind. The man's gaze dropped, giving Harris the perfect opportunity to strike him in the windpipe, followed by a quick jab to the kidney, before knocking him out cold with an elbow to the temple. The man lay sprawled on the floor, unconscious. Harris couldn't be certain how long he would stay that way or if the noise had attracted any unwanted attention.

Harris approached the girl cautiously, his eyes assessing her injuries.

"Are you alright? Are you hurt?"

The girl recoiled, fear still evident in her eyes.

"Don't worry, I won't harm you. I just want to make sure you're not injured."

She stared at him, trembling, unable to utter a word. Harris felt a sense of helplessness. He couldn't abandon her in this vulnerable state. Thinking on his feet, he removed his flannel over shirt and handed it to the girl.

"Here, you can use this to cover yourself."

Still silent, the girl took the shirt and wrapped it around her shoulders.

"I'm Doc, what's your name?" Still not speaking, she ceased trembling, her posture straightening. "You can't stay here, you know. Once your friend wakes up, he won't be pleased. If you stay, you might end up lost forever."

The girl's attention was captured, and she stood up, her shoulders squared.

"Do you think it will be any better for me when I return after this?"

She finally met Harris' gaze, revealing a deeper fear than just the bruises on her body.

"You have no idea what you've done. He may have beaten me, but they will kill me. Not only will I be unable to work with my face like this, but I don't have payment for today. Word will spread that he withheld payment because I planned to rob him."

Her words hit Harris hard, and he finally understood the gravity of the situation.

Harris reached in his wallet and took what cash he had left out. He knew it was more than what she would have been paid, but he felt he owed it to her.

"Take this, give them your fee. Do what you like with the rest. Tell them he was drunk and passed out. It isn't much, but it should keep you out of trouble for now."

"Why are you giving this to me. I won't do anything for you," she said almost defiantly.

Harris looked at her softly, lowering his voice to almost a whisper. "I don't want anything from you. I'm sorry I can't do more to help you. Once there was someone I could have helped, should have helped, and well, she wouldn't be much older than you are if I had. I hope someone would do the same for her."

Harris turned to leave, tears burning the backs of his eyes.

"May, my name is May,"

| 9 |

CHAPTER 9

DAPHNE, JUNE 2008

It hadn't taken Daphne long to realize that the stardom she was ac-quiring wasn't the kind little girls stayed up at night dreaming of. It wasn't made of the fantasies that filled her journal or the idle gossip that filled the air on the playground. This type of popularity streaked her face with tears, woke her when she was able to sleep with violent shaking. It was filled with dirt that soap wouldn't wash away and pain that stabbed at her soul.

Nila had spent the entire ride from Daphne's neighborhood to the small apartment talking about costumes, make-up, and lighting. She had painted a glamorous picture of her studio and the portfolio she was going to build for Daphne. Nila had been so excited that day, al-most more than Daphne. They had chatted too much that Daphne didn't realize that they had driven far longer than a drive downtown should take, even with traffic. That was something else Daphne failed to notice until it was too late. There had been no tall buildings, no traffic lights, not really any other cars at all since they left the small town.

Looking back now, Daphne realized how much she had missed that day. All the little things that shouldn't have added up. However, in all her excitement, with all the attention, the little details had evaded her. Nila was good at distracting you from seeing what was right in front of your eyes. Even now, after Daphne knew the truth, had experienced the truth, Nila had a way of talking around it. She made the evilness of it all seem like everyday life. Just going through the motions, as if it were as simple as checking off a box on one of those chore lists Daphne's mom had hanging in the kitchen.

There were so many girls at the cheer camp that day, why had Daphne been so accepting that she was any more special than the rest of them? Why had she not questioned how Nila had found her at the back of her subdivision? The story of driving around looking for her, that certainly was true, but Daphne had thought she was smart. Why did she not remember the van was already gone when she left? Then there was the call to her mom. Her mom would never agree to let her go off with some stranger. Would she? Was anyone even looking for her anymore?

Nila had only kept her at the apartment for two days, long enough to finish editing the actual cheer pictures for the camp director. Daphne had watched as pictures of that day filled the computer, her friends flashing across the screen one by one. Even the pictures of Daphne were edited and packaged with care, the last happy memories she had, forever memorialized.

The apartment was a small studio with heavy curtains covering the three windows. It was on the third floor, and Daphne never heard anyone else coming or going from next door or across the hall. There was no television or radio, just a row of books, some magazines that were months old, a small bed, a couch, and a dining room table that Nila used as a desk. In the corner, there was a camera set up on a tripod with two studio lights, a few different backdrops, and some props. That was one of the few things Nila had been truthful about.

There was a ton of makeup and costumes, and she had taken enough photographs of Daphne for a portfolio. Daphne hoped no one ever saw those pictures, but it wasn't long before she knew that was the least of her fears.

Daphne had barely slept those first nights. Her eyes took in everything around her, looking for anything to help her get away. She listened for any sound that could signal an end to this nightmare. Nila had planned for everything. There was enough to eat and drink, clothes for Daphne, toiletries, and locks on everything. They never had to leave that tiny space. Daphne was never alone, not to shower, go to the bathroom, or sleep. At night, she was given a sleeping bag to lie on, her ankles tightly locked together with plastic ties that had to be cut each day. One wrist was cuffed tightly to Nila's.

On the third day, Nila had thrown fresh clothing at Daphne. When she was dressed, Nila combed her hair, braiding it into two neat rows on either side of Daphne's head. Nila had applied a small amount of makeup to her eyes and lips before throwing everything of importance into large trash bags. They were going on a trip; she had told her. A part of Daphne that had grown numb started to tingle, to come alive. A trip meant the van. The van meant the road, and the road meant people. People who were certainly looking for her. Daphne knew they had driven farther than she had expected, and she wasn't paying much attention, but after the clouds had cleared, the sun was still far in the sky, so they hadn't gone too far. They were certainly close enough for people to be looking.

Nila had the package with the cheer photographs too, which meant she was taking them somewhere. There wasn't any postage on them, so maybe there was still hope for Daphne yet. There was still time for Daphne to be smart. She would pay attention this time and wouldn't let herself be distracted by Nila. If there was an opportunity to get away, to get somebody's attention, to get help, Daphne had to wait for it and see it. Daphne had to be ready.

That morning, she did exactly as she was told. She did everything she could to keep her head down and her eyes from wandering. The trip to the van was quick. Nila's grip on Daphne's shoulder was so tight it would leave marks for days. Once inside the van, Nila put the plastic ties around Daphne's wrists and feet, but instead of buckling her in, Nila closed the door and walked to the back of the van. Daphne heard the rear doors open, then shut. A few seconds later, Nila's hands were under Daphne's, pulling her backward to the rear. Nila positioned Daphne so she was lying on her side. Nila used another plastic tie to secure the ties around Daphne's wrists to the ties around her ankles.

Now that Daphne was in a half backbend, lying on her side, Nila knelt down next to her. She pulled something from her back pocket and unfolded it, a small smile on her face as she turned it toward Daphne. It was a picture of her family taken during spring break, the one of them at the beach together. Tears started to fall from Daphne's eyes as fear sunk in. When Nila spoke, her tone was flat and even, with no emotion at all.

"You know what this is, don't you, Daphne 10 ½?" The question came out more as a statement. "Of course, you do, smart girl. That is why you are going to be a good girl. No noise, no moving, just quiet."

Daphne swallowed down her sobs as she nodded her head in agreement. Nila gave Daphne a quick pat on the cheek before hopping in the driver's seat.

Daphne lay motionless the entire ride, as silent as possible. Even when they pulled up to the Y and she could hear the squawk of the police radio and the voice of her coach as Nila handed over the package. Daphne lay there frozen in fear, desperately trying to stay hidden. Nila got back in the van and as they drove away, Daphne let out a breath. That picture used to be in a frame next to her parents' bed, and now Nila had it. Nila had her; there was no escaping. All Daphne could do was stare at the back of the woman who betrayed her, the woman with a small scar on her shoulder that looked like a broken heart.

***

Shane searched the house in a flurry, screaming for Daphne. Panic filled his lungs with each unanswered call. He didn't remember making the calls to his parents, nor could he recall how long he had sat on the floor in front of the door. Tears flooded his face as he just stared out the open door, looking for a tiny figure to come bouncing up the driveway. Shane had rehearsed the speech he planned to give Daphne a hundred times in his mind, but with each passing minute, the words slipped away, replaced with pleading for her to be okay.

Shane's father was the first to come through the door. Shane wasn't sure what he had said to him. His father retraced Shane's steps, working his way room by room, shouting for his daughter. Shane didn't bother to stop him, even at fourteen he understood it was something his father needed to do. So, Shane just sat on the floor, watching, waiting, pleading.

Shane's mother arrived a short time later, more frantic than his father had been. There had been phone calls between his parents since his dad finished his search of the home. Shane was vaguely aware of spouting out answers to questions. More phone calls were made to friends, to the Y, Daphne's coach. His parents were rushing past him in a blur. No one had really talked to him yet. They had asked when he got home, when he got to the Y, who he had talked to. But they hadn't really talked to him. For that, Shane was grateful. What could he say? Daphne was missing, and it was all his fault.

The police arrived a few hours later. They walked around the house, taking in every detail. It was unnerving and infuriating at the same time. His dad filled out a statement while his mom gave details of what Daphne was wearing. More officers started arriving, and a tall man with stripes on his sleeve started barking orders at them. Soon, the entire neighborhood was lit up with blue and red lights.

At some point in the evening, a woman joined the officers. She wore pants and a polo, her badge hanging around her neck, and Shane could see a gun fixed to her hip under a windbreaker. The woman, who introduced herself as Detective Morris, was the first person to speak to Shane since this nightmare started. Detective Morris sank down on the floor next to Shane. Sitting there, staring out the door with Shane, she didn't say anything for several minutes.

"This isn't your fault, kid. You didn't make this happen; you couldn't have known."

Shane understood what she was trying to say. But if the detective had known how he had taken his time at the field, how he had slowed down when the storm started out of spite, she would probably slap the cuffs on him and throw away the key.

"We have some of the smartest and bravest people out there looking for your sister. If she is out there, they will find her. You are her big brother, and whether you know it or not, you probably know her better than anyone. Anything you can tell me can help me send my people in the right place. I've talked to your parents, and they told me what was supposed to happen today. They told me what the coach told them, but I have a brother too, and I know we have secrets that we keep for each other. Secrets we don't tell our parents or even our friends. Shane, I need you to tell me the secrets you and Daphne have."

The detective sat quietly next to Shane while he spilled everything from that day. She wasn't angry or judging him. She just listened, taking it all in, thinking. When Shane was finished, he looked over at

Detective Morris, expecting the worst, but instead, he saw compassion in her eyes, understanding.

"Shane, thank you for telling me all this. It is very helpful. The coach said Daphne told her she was supposed to walk home with a friend, then ran off toward your neighborhood. She had seen a couple of kids farther up the road, so she didn't think anything about it. She was the last one there and had already locked up for the day, so she left. Shane, it had just started raining when she pulled out of the Y. Do you understand what I am saying?"

Shane just looked at her, not quite understanding what he was missing.

Shane shook his head slowly, still letting the words tumble around in his mind.

"Shane, Daphne walked off before you would normally get there to pick her up. It wouldn't have mattered. She would have been gone already no matter what. The camp let out early because of the approaching storm. The thing is, we identified one of the girls the coach saw as being one of Daphne's friends. We talked to her, and she said Daphne did not walk with her. She never even saw Daphne after leaving the Y. She also said she doesn't remember any cars passing either. The other girl walking with her said the same thing. That is where we are stuck. If Daphne didn't catch up to them, and no one picked her up off the street, where did she end up?"

Shane was still thinking about the timing, about how the camp had let out early. His brain not wanting to accept that there was nothing he could have done to help his little sister. He was supposed to be there, he should have been there, and he wasn't. Now Daphne was out there somewhere, his family heartbroken, and he couldn't do anything to fix it.

"The cut-through," the words came out in a whisper, so quiet Shane wasn't even sure he had said them out loud.

"There is a cut-through. A path that goes through the wooded area and comes out behind the houses in our neighborhood. There are two paths at the end, the first one brings you right to our street and the other circles around to the back of the neighborhood. I've taken her with me a few times, but mom doesn't want us using it, so I stopped taking it."

"But does Daphne know about it? Would she take it if it was about to rain?"

The detective was already on her feet as Shane shook his head, a flicker of hope in both their eyes. Detective Morris got on her radio to inform the K9 officers about the route and the two paths while Shane stood up. His parents walked towards him, anxiously waiting to hear what the commotion was about. The three of them stood together, holding tight to the little bit of hope they had just unearthed.

A short time later, Detective Morris walked back through the door. Shane hadn't realized that he had been expecting Daphne to be with her until he saw that the detective was alone.

"We didn't find anything on the cut-through or either path. With the heavy rain earlier, it isn't surprising though. The dogs can only do so much under the best circumstances, and with the pathways being washed out, any scent that would have been left behind was also washed away. Officers are still out there. However, we did find something between two houses at the back of the neighborhood. It was near where the last path would have ended."

Detective Morris produced a small pompom attached to a clip.

"Do any of you recognize this? I know Daphne is into cheer."

They all looked at it, studying it like a precious gem. Shane's parents both shook their heads, indicating that they didn't recognize it.

Shane's mother spoke in between fresh onset of sobs, "No, I don't know what that is. It isn't her cheer team colors or her school colors."

Detective Morris was speaking now, asking about a recent photo and talking about updating the BOLO that was issued earlier.

Now it was Shane's father talking, "BOLO? What is that? What about an Amber Alert?"

"A BOLO, or Be On The Lookout, is a description of Daphne issued to all local law enforcement. Our officers, along with adjacent agencies, will continue looking. We are canvassing the neighborhood, talking to everyone, looking for any cameras that may have caught your daughter walking past. We don't issue Amber Alerts as an agency. That is done through the US Department of Justice when a child under 17 goes missing under certain circumstances. Right now, unfortunately, we do not have enough information to submit for an Amber Alert."

"My little girl is missing. She is a ten-year-old little girl, out there somewhere. We don't know what happened to her, if someone has her, if she is lost, if she is hurt, and you are telling me that doesn't meet some criteria?"

Shane's father was gritting his teeth to keep from yelling, the raw emotion bursting with each syllable.

"That is exactly the problem, Mr. Harris. We don't know what happened to her yet. For an Amber Alert, we need information not only about your daughter but also about the abduction. Right now, we don't even know if there was an abduction. I promise you, we are looking, and if we get to that point, we will get it out there. As hard as it is to hear, it is just as hard to say. We need time to do our job."

Detective Morris was doing her best to be firm and caring, a speech she had probably given to many parents many times. Shane's eyes went back to the tiny bobble in the detective's hand. Something she had said to him earlier echoed in his head. "You are her big brother."

"Can I see that again?" Shane asked, gesturing toward the pompom.

The detective opened her hand and let it dangle in front of him. Of course, he didn't know why he hadn't realized before.

"The colors, they are my team colors. Well, not my team yet, but the high school I am starting. I am going out for the baseball team. That's why I started camp this summer. Those are the school colors. Daphne asked me if baseball games had cheerleaders. I told her I didn't think so, and she told me it was a shame; every team needed a cheerleader."

In the days that followed the revelation that Daphne had made it into the neighborhood, everyone had been questioned and re-questioned. Rumors about neighbors spread like wildfire. Everyone had a theory about what happened to the little girl who never came home. Newspapers ran story after story, even the local news was showing Daphne's picture. They still had no idea what happened to her, only hunches and ideas. They speculated that she had gotten lost on the path because of the rain, then took the last exit. Others thought maybe someone grabbed her on the path, and the pompom was dropped after in a getaway. Then there were others who said that it hadn't been Daphne's at all.

They had set up a command post at the Y since that was Daphne's last known location. Tip lines were set up, and a reward for information had been posted. Shane had been questioned multiple times over the last few days, as if miraculously the day's events were going to change. His parents were questioned too. Their alibis were checked and rechecked. Most people were kind, wanting to help any way they could, but others had already decided his parents had done something sinister. Shane spent his nights in Daphne's room and his days at the Y. A search party was being organized, and he was going to be a part of it. Detective Morris was supportive of his need to do something, to feel like he was a part of it all.

That morning, she had called him and asked him how he was doing. His parents were arguing in the background over something stupid. She told him this was normal in times of stress like this. Detective Morris told him they wanted to do another press conference, but this time they wanted to include Shane if he was up for it. She told him there would not be any questions or press, just a recording of Shane making a statement about his sister. They were planning to send it to the media as a release from the department. They wanted to use the Y as a backdrop. Shane agreed, and Detective Morris made arrangements to pick him up and bring him to the Y.

On the way to the Y, Detective Morris talked to Shane as if he were a person, not just some kid. Shane needed that. At home, he felt invisible, like an afterthought. His parents whispered behind closed doors or changed the subject every time he walked into the room. At night, he could hear his father pacing and his mother crying. It was all so overwhelming. Detective Morris understood; she just let him talk.

"Son of a bitch!"

Shane jolted at the sudden interruption and pain as the detective's arm caught him across the chest when she slammed on the brakes. Just as they were turning into the Y, a van had pulled out, cutting in front of them.

"Well, that will get the heart going quicker than caffeine. Are you okay?"

Shane let out a breath and shook his head.

"Yeah, I'm good. Thanks."

The detective made the turn into the parking lot as Shane stared after the van, which was fading into the distance.

| 10 |

CHAPTER 10

CRANE, JANUARY 2022

Crane was abruptly interrupted by the sound of two girls engaged in a heated argument upstairs. The incessant bickering between the sisters seemed to have no end; if one claimed the sky was blue, the other vehemently insisted it was a shade of azure. They could find a reason to argue about anything under the sun. Despite the lack of urgency in their voices and the normalcy of this morning ritual, Crane couldn't shake the unsettling feeling that crept up her spine

Winter had settled in, even in the warmth of Florida, where the outside temperature fluctuated between the pleasant high sixties and low seventies. Yet, an inexplicable chill ran through Crane's body, causing her to instinctively rub her arms in a feeble attempt to generate some warmth and ward off the goosebumps that adorned her skin. No matter how vigorously she rubbed her sweater-clad arms, the comforting embrace of heat eluded her.

With each insult hurled between the sisters, the knot in Crane's stomach tightened. She despised witnessing their fights but understood that it was an inevitable part of sisterhood during this tender age. However, something felt different about this morning, about this particular argument. Crane struggled to pinpoint the exact cause of her unease. It wasn't the words they exchanged; it was something far more profound, lurking beneath the surface.

With one last inaudible yell, the air hung heavy before the distinct sound of a door slamming reverberated through the house. Crane's heightened senses picked up the echo of their mother's exhausted sigh from the kitchen, where the scent of breakfast lingered in the air. An unexplained urgency propelled Crane to investigate what had stirred such anger in the family at such an early hour.

Treading the stairs, Crane could feel a surge of panic welling up inside her with each step. Midway, she abandoned caution and took two stairs at a time, the chill that had gripped her earlier now replaced by beads of sweat. Reaching the landing, the sound of the shower starting in the hall bath guided her towards the closed door that had unleashed the commotion driving her upstairs. Crane rapped on the door, but silence greeted her. Her heart pounded faster; her chest constricted. She attempted to turn the handle, but it stubbornly refused to yield.

Pure panic consumed Crane; a sense of foreboding settled deep within her, yet she couldn't grasp its source. She tightened her grip on the handle and summoned every ounce of strength to push against the door. Finally, it swung open, revealing an empty room with a meticulously made bed. Crane scoured the room, desperate to find the younger sister. Her calls echoed unanswered, and the girl seemed to have vanished into thin air. A sudden presence loomed behind Crane, and then she heard the haunting voice.

"She isn't here. She's never here."

Crane turned and saw Angel staring back at her. There was a loud ringing in her ears suddenly. Crane felt the world crumbling around her as the noise grew louder. She reached for her gun as Angel lunged toward her.

Crane sat up drenched and shaking. The alarm still blaring from her phone. Murch was perched at the end of the bed, waiting for her to signal him. Crane silenced the alarm and patted the space next to her on the bed. Murch quickly jumped up and began to lick the tears from her face, nuzzling her neck until her heartrate regulated.

It had been a long time since Crane had that nightmare. It was always the same, except Angel. Angel was different.

***

The drive to the office failed to alleviate the lingering anxiety that consumed Crane. Her morning routine had become monotonous, almost robotic. Even Murch, her faithful running companion, seemed disappointed during their morning jog. The route remained unchanged, and the weather was typical for the season, yet every step felt arduous, as if her muscles were weighed down. The nightmare she had awoken from had shattered her serenity, and Crane still grappled with the urgency that had consumed her in the dream.

This particular nightmare had plagued her for countless years. She had poured her heart out to therapists and psychiatrists, discussing it at length. Her mother was aware of her troubled sleep, but Crane shielded her from the intricate details, not wanting to burden her with pain and worry. In truth, outside of clinical sessions, Crane confided in only one person about the intimate intricacies of her nightmare, but he had fled as soon as he had the chance. Since then, Crane kept her torment to herself.

Of course, she engaged in conversations about work with her team and partner, Adams. Those discussions were different, for they revolved around shared experiences, moments that bound them together. Such talks helped them navigate the most challenging cases, allowing them to maintain a clear distinction between work and a blissful home life. But the dream was distinct; it belonged solely to Crane, a burden she carried alone.

Any hopes that the twenty-minute hot shower and extra foundation covered her restless night disappeared with the look on Adams face when she walked in the office.

"Rough night huh?" It came out as more of a statement than a question.

When Crane didn't respond, Vickers turned around, a slight smirk on his face. Something in Crane's eyes must have caught his attention, as the smirk was quickly replaced by a faint concerned scowl.

"You feeling alright kiddo? You know my rule about bringing the crud into the office."

"I feel fine. Just didn't get much sleep. Must have been a cat in the yard or something. Murch must have woken me ten times to go out."

Crane felt a slight twinge of guilt blaming her zombie appearance on her faithful K9, but she didn't feel like going into detail or arguing about if she had a flu shot yet. She made a mental note to give him an extra treat when she got home tonight.

Crane fired up her computers, ready to conquer the day ahead. As she brewed a fresh pot of coffee, she couldn't help but reflect on yesterday's late-night efforts to complete Angel's arrest packet. Vickers, her supervisor, had urged her to come in later, playing the role of a concerned father. But Crane knew it was more about the overtime she had accumulated this pay period. With a steaming cup of coffee in hand, she settled into her workstation, logging into her various screens, determined to shake off the morning uneasiness.

"Anything new with the case?"

Lost in her own world, Crane hadn't noticed Adams trying to get her attention. When she finally turned to look at him, she saw that he had turned his chair towards her, his screensaver displaying a slideshow of his family. The current picture was from Halloween, capturing his daughters dressed up as firefighters. They looked absolutely thrilled, while their father stood behind them, unable to hide his disapproval. Crane found it to be a priceless moment, encapsulating the essence of family life. It also meant that his computer had been idle for a few minutes now, stuck in the cuteness overload slideshow.

"Is that a genuine question or just the next phase of observation?" Crane quipped in response.

Adams was somewhat of a profiler, having studied psychology and human behavior in college. He had big plans for a career with the FBI and the Behavioral Analysis Unit, but he found love which led to marriage and babies. They were lucky to have him but damn he could be irritating when he turned those skills on you.

"It's a common question from one coworker to another after they spent weeks on a case."

"Maybe, but you are far from common, and you know everything I know about the case, maybe more. So, Detective Adams, what is the real question?"

Crane met Adams' intense gaze with her own narrowed, inquisitive eyes. Time seemed to stand still as they engaged in this silent yet intense staring contest. Finally, Adams couldn't contain his amusement any longer and broke into a warm smile. Crane reciprocated the gesture before returning her attention to the multiple screens in front of her, desperately trying to regain her focus. Something gnawed at her, but she couldn't quite pinpoint what it was. The unsettling dream she had the previous night had left her disoriented, making it nearly impossible to think clearly. Normally, it took her no more than thirty minutes, or at most forty-five, to complete a report. Yet, here she was, an hour into it, and still far from finished.

It was nearing lunch time and the guys were talking over which place they were going to hit up. Crane was rewatching the video of her interview with Angel for the second time. She was missing something and she knew it. Angel had to be the key. Her dream was always the same, but last night one thing had changed. Angel. Angel was there. It was possible that the arrest had been on her mind when she went to sleep, causing him to invade her most intimate thoughts, but there was something about his presence that told her to look deeper. So here she was, watching, listening, rewinding, pausing.

Crane was about to give up and change directions when she heard it. It hadn't mattered to the arrest or the charges so she hadn't pressed him on it. They had already written several search warrants for apps they found on his tablet, but it could be weeks before anything came back. Crane needed to talk to Angel now. He had been booked late last night and it wasn't quite noon yet. Angel may not have had his first appearance yet, and if he had he might not have counsel still.

"Hey, did Angel ever lawyer up?"

Adams and Vickers looked at her like she was speaking in tongues. She was already dialing the jail to ensure Angel was still there and available for interview. Even if he had, what she wanted to know more about wouldn't affect his current charges. She would have to tread lightly because anything incriminating, he said regarding this case or future charges could be inadmissible, but she had to give it a shot. She needed to more about the process, they already had him dead to rights on those charges, he already talked about the important things, so what she wanted to hear about wouldn't matter to the case. Not in the grand scheme of things anyway.

"Not that I am aware of, but he was probably assigned a public defender if he had his first appearance already."

Crane grabbed her stuff, "Well cross your fingers he didn't and he is in the mood to talk."

***

Less than thirty minutes later, Crane was standing in line to go through the metal detectors at the side entrance and the county jail. Angel had gotten himself put in safe booking not long after processing last night, missing initial appearance for the morning. Supposedly Angel had a nervous breakdown, leading jail staff to isolate him overnight for his own safety. He would either see a judge later this afternoon or tomorrow morning. He had twenty-four to forty-eight hours to be seen in the state of Florida. Crane had been advised that he had been released back to general population after lunch so she a very short window to speak with him if he got on the docket for afternoon appearances.

Crane was escorted through the jail and upstairs to the area that held the mail inmates awaiting court. Crane took her seat in the enclosure set in the middle of the pod. It was a small space, surrounded by bars, a small metal table and two round metal seats, one on each side, securely bolted to the ground. Crane pulled out her small recording device, a note pad and pen while she waited for Angel to be brought to her.

A few minutes later, dressed in an orange jump suite, white socks and black slides, Angel came into view. He was escorted by a correction's officer she recognized from her numerous previous visits. Angels' hair was disheveled, his eyes red and puffy, his shoulders slumped, a sharp contrast to the cocky man she spoke with yesterday. Reality had settled in for Angel and what his future held. That could either work for or against Crane.

The officer indicated for Angel to sit in front of Crane and to put his hands on the small table. Angel's hand restraints were then looped through the hinge on the table to secure him in place. The door was shut and locked, and now they were face to face, alone and staring at each other.

Crane took a minute to look over Angel, to get an idea of where she was at with him, where he was at mentally. She had to play this just right if she was going to get him to talk, to give her the answers she needed. Crane pressed a button on the side of the recorder, beginning to archive their interaction.

"Hi Angel. I'm sure you remember me from yesterday, I am Detective Crane. I wanted to talk to you about a few things that we already spoke about, things that don't really have any effect on the status of your current charges. I am going to record this conversation for my own notes. I know you are aware of your rights as I read them to you yesterday, but I can read them again if you like. Do mind speaking with me?"

Crane tried her best to remain open and friendly with her tone. Try-ing even harder not to hold her breath waiting for Angel to respond. She could feel her heart begin to race but she didn't break her gaze. Angel just looked back, almost looking through her. She thought he was going to tell her to go to hell, but something in his eyes said he welcomed the visit, even if it was from the police.

"You already put me in jail. What else do you want? You say it won't change anything so why would it matter to you? This is some kind of trick."

"No, Angel there is no trick. I just need to ask you if you have been as-signed legal counsel if you understand your rights and if you are will-ing to talk to me today. No tricks, just questions. I don't think you just decided one day to do the things you did. I don't think you ever wanted to hurt your niece, it just happened, right? But that isn't what I want to talk to you about."

Crane didn't want to press to hard until he agreed to speak to her, until he stated he knew his rights and was willing to talk with her. It was like walking a tight rope, knowing there was a net but not being able to see it. They had the warrants already but she didn't have the time nor was she certain they would give her what she was looking for. Crane knew Angel could. She needed him.

"I only ever loved her, my niece. She is so beautiful, so delicate. I wanted to show her what love felt like. What my love felt like."

"I understand, she is precious. It is obvious that you love her very much. I can't continue this conversation, I'll have to leave, if you don't answer my questions."

Crane tried to sound sympathetic, looking at him as compassionately as she could. She started picking things up, as if packing to leave, in hopes it would get Angel's attention. She moved slowly and intentionally, waiting for him to say something, afraid to make eye contact.

"I understand, you can stay. I will tell you what you want. Just tell me how my angel is?"

Crane paused, breathing slowly, putting things back in place. She was biding time as she gained her composure before speaking or looking up. When she was confident the emotion was gone from her voice and expression she began.

"I haven't seen her, but from what I have been told she is doing fine. Like I said, that isn't what I want to talk to you about though. I want to ask you about the videos. Not the videos we found, about the ones you mentioned when we talked yesterday, the ones that we didn't find. The ones that I explained, if they are what you say they are, can't get you in any trouble."

"Why do you want to know about that? I already told you; they were just regular pictures. The website would email them to me, then I had to take a video of myself jerking off to them. Then send that video back to them to get the real porn. The porn that you found. I uploaded the videos directly so I don't have them. I didn't save the emails because like I said, they were just regular pictures. Kids yes, but they weren't doing anything. They had clothes on."

"You said regular pictures, what does that mean? I know you said they were clothed and not doing anything but what kind of pictures of kids were they?"

"Just kids. I don't know. Like one's parents take."

"So just family pictures of kids?"

"No, not like that. Like the school pictures you have to buy. Or like baseball pictures, or cheerleader. You know like when you kid is in some activity and they have their picture taken. Some of them were like that kind you buy, but some you could tell the kids were just wearing the costume."

"What makes you say that? About them wearing a costume?"

"Because over time, I would see different kids but the same uniform or outfit. Some pictures you could tell were older and some newer, but the same clothes. So, I knew they weren't real uniforms."

"How did you know about this website? I'm sure you didn't just search for it online."

"In a chatroom, on one of those regular porn sites. People talk sometimes, but it is sort of like code. They have bots that look for that kind of talk so they break up the words and stuff."

"I know about that. Do you know who it was? The person who mentioned it?"

"No. They don't use names in places like that. There was a handle that would pop up every now and then with an email address. Always different email and name. The name similar all the time though. I can't remember it. Something with tattoos or art."

"Thank you, Angel, you have been very helpful."

Crane drove back to the station, a new sense of focus and drive filling her veins. He may have deleted the pictures but they were still there, and there was still a device they haven't found, the one he used record and upload those videos. Even if he directly uploaded them, there would be a trace of it, and they hadn't found any. They had to get back in the house.

| 11 |

CHAPTER 11

VANESSA, CHRISTMAS 2009

Vanessa never wanted to see a camera again as long as she lived, a wish she knew was only a thought in her mind now that reality was settling in. After two days, she was permitted to take a shower, with the door open and Nila poised at the door. Vanessa would have used the entire bar of soap, attempting to scour her skin off clean to the bone if Nila had given her more than five minutes to clean herself and wash her hair.

Even after scrubbing as hard as she could under the scalding water, Vanessa felt just as dirty as she had before stepping into the small bath. The labels on the various bottles of shampoo and conditioner offered aromas of vanilla and roses, but all she could smell was filth. The kind of stench that has no origin, the kind that just hangs in the air like a thick cloud.

It was Christmas Day, but there were no signs of celebration. No twinkling tree adorned with ornaments, no presents waiting to be unwrapped, and no tantalizing aroma of ham wafting from the oven. Vanessa longed to hear Abigail's playful voice echoing through the halls, teasing her as she had done countless times before. She had deliberately suppressed any thoughts of the ballet or the Sugar Plum Fairy costume she had donned with such pride just days earlier. The memory of that afternoon now made her stomach churn, threatening to bring bile to the surface.

She was tired from having to sleep on the floor, tied to the rail of the footboard in Nila's small bedroom. The apartment was barely furnished, with no personal items other than clothing indicating it was occupied. There was a small dining room table with two chairs, a love seat, and a makeshift photography studio set up in the corner. The apartment was small and dark, with the two windows covered with thick curtains. There was no television or radio, providing no link to the outside world.

Vanessa should have known something was wrong that afternoon when Nila mentioned she needed to stop by her apartment to grab a bulb for her light on the way to the studio. The drive to the apartment was forty-five minutes, hardly "on the way," and why would Nila keep supplies at her house instead of her studio? Vanessa had been such an idiot.

When they arrived at the apartment, Nila told Vanessa to come inside because she didn't feel right leaving her alone in the car. They walked around several buildings that all looked the same before climbing up three flights of stairs at the entrance to one. Vanessa caught a glimpse over the rail before they entered the apartment. There was a parking area like the one they had just left, with several open spots. Vanessa didn't think it was odd that Nila had not parked there until it was too late.

As soon as she stepped inside, everything transformed. The door stood before her, adorned with multiple locks, each demanding its own unique key. The once warm and compassionate Nila had undergone an abrupt transformation, her demeanor turning icy as she barked orders. Vanessa found herself being shuffled into different outfits, forced to strike poses that made her feel more like a vulnerable child than a budding model. Some shots captured her in compromising positions, while others exploited her innocence. At one point, Vanessa mustered the courage to voice her discomfort, only to be met with Nila's dismissive reply that she had yet to experience true discomfort. The chilling tone in which Nila uttered those words sent shivers down Vanessa's spine.

Despite Nila's seemingly impenetrable facade, Vanessa detected a subtle tension in her jaw, as if she were suppressing something. Avoiding eye contact, Nila seemed to possess an uncanny understanding of Vanessa's emotions, as if she knew exactly what the young girl was going through and what awaited her next. This realization should have provided a glimmer of solace, but instead, it intensified Vanessa's fear. She had been so focused on concealing her terror, but now it felt futile. Vanessa couldn't help but wonder if Nila, too, had once been a frightened soul on the other side of the camera.

***

"Abby? Abby? Abigail? Can you hear me? Did you catch what I just said?"

Caught up in her emotions, Abigail had completely forgotten she was still clutching the phone, her dad's voice echoing on the other end. Tears blurred her vision so much that she couldn't even see through the windshield anymore. It wasn't until a blaring car horn startled her that she snapped back to reality, back to the parking lot, back inside her car, gripping the phone, while her dad informed her that Nessy was missing. Instantly, sobs choked her throat, making it difficult to breathe. The world spun around her, leaving her feeling disoriented and dizzy.

"Abby, please tell me where you are. I'll send someone to pick you up and bring you home. Your mom will be there soon, and I'm on my way. The police have been contacted, and they'll need to talk to you. Abby, are you still with me? Let me know your location."

Her dad's voice had transitioned from panic to a more composed and steady tone, the kind he used in court. Abigail began to steady her breathing, following the technique she learned from her time on the track team. Inhale, exhale, in through the nose, out through the mouth, slowing her racing heart. After a minute, the sobs started to fade, and she regained a sense of awareness, the tingling and haziness dissipating.

"I am at the shopping plaza downtown, the one by the hospital. I am sitting in my car in front of the pizza place on the corner."

As her dad engaged in a conversation, presumably on his work phone, his voice resonated with a sense of urgency. Yet, his tone remained unwavering, emanating strength and composure. Abigail eagerly awaited, her senses heightened, marveling at her dad's ability to maintain his cool amidst tense situations. Her mother often attributed Abigail's inquisitive nature and keen observation skills to her dad's influence. If only they could witness her now, clutching the phone with white-knuckled hands, tears streaming down her face, her body trembling uncontrollably. Oh, why had she been so unkind that morning? Why had she arrived late at the ballet studio? Why hadn't she asked more questions instead of making assumptions?

Just as her dad was about to resume the conversation, a patrol car pulled up behind her vehicle, its vibrant lights oscillating between shades of blue and red, the siren wailing in the distance. Her dad assured her that the officers would be by her side shortly, ready to escort her back home. While she hastily concluded the call, two officers swiftly closed in on her, their presence becoming more apparent with each passing moment.

One officer drove her home in the patrol car, while the other followed in Abigail's car. Abby wasn't sure if the silent drive was because of the situation or because her dad was a judge, maybe a combination of both. Abby was sure it was the latter that had gotten them to her location so quickly. Being the daughter of a sitting judge had its perks, especially when he was once the district attorney. It also helped that her mother was a well-known attorney in the city.

Abigail was playing the entire day over and over again in her head when they made the turn onto her street. The entire road was lit up with red and blue lights. Marked and unmarked police cars were parked on both sides of the road, in driveways, and in the grass. Neighbors had come out to try and catch a glimpse of what was happening. Abigail knew her parents' notoriety meant a strong media presence was forthcoming. As her family home grew near, the silence of the ride was finally broken.

"The detective is already inside with your parents. Another detective is on the way. We don't know who has your sister or why she was taken, but know we are all doing everything to find those answers."

Abigail could hear the grief in the officer's voice. He wore a gold band on the ring finger of his left hand. It wasn't shiny and new, but it didn't show signs of years of wear. Abigail figured he had probably been with the department for five or more years for her father to trust him, probably married for about the same. This meant he most likely had a kid or two of his own at home. His emotions and statement were likely genuine, but Abigail doubted he would be the one to give her the answers she needed. She thanked him and made her way inside, longing for the warmth of her parents' embrace. A thought that sent sudden jolt of guilt straight to her soul.

****

Vanessa knew that people were out looking for her, a lot of people by now. She wasn't sure how long Nila had watched her before taking her from the studio. She was sure that it wasn't a spontaneous act; it had been thought out, planned, maybe for her specifically or just any girl at the studio. Vanessa couldn't shake the feeling that this wasn't random, though. The clothing she was given wasn't a perfect fit, but it was too close to be bought for just anyone. Why her? Was it because of who she was? But then why the pictures, and why had there been no call, like in the movies? Maybe it was a coincidence; she had been a last-minute replacement, and she had been picked as the replacement because she had been so similar in size. Maybe it was mistaken identity?

That didn't make sense either, though. If they had meant to take another girl, they would have gotten rid of Vanessa already or simply not have taken her in the first place. Nila knew when she started taking the pictures at the studio that she was there because the original girl had to drop out. Everything had been last minute; how would Nila have known? Vanessa watched Nila as much as she could without being obvious.

With purposeful determination, Nila orchestrated every move, leaving nothing to chance. She was meticulous, always armed with a plan within a plan. Gone were the days of lighthearted conversations and playful banter between Nila and Vanessa. Instead, their interactions now consisted solely of demands and instructions. Nila seemed to have shed her humanity, leaving Vanessa longing for the person she once knew.

As Vanessa observed Nila methodically packing their belongings into oversized garbage bags, a sense of unease washed over her. Their imminent departure filled her with a mix of anticipation and dread. How far were the pursuers willing to go to find her? How long would they persist in their search? Time was slipping away, and Vanessa felt the weight of urgency bearing down on her. Every move she made was under constant surveillance, leaving her feeling trapped and helpless.

"Here, put these on," Nila urged, handing Vanessa a set of clothes. "A car will be here soon to take us away. There are people waiting for you."

Overwhelmed by the situation, Vanessa's mind raced, trying to process the gravity of the moment. She swiftly dressed in the unfamiliar attire while Nila gathered her old clothes and stowed them away. As Nila approached, she set down her backpack and knelt beside Vanessa. With a torn piece of tape in her hand, Nila secured Vanessa's wrists together, followed by her feet, and finally placed a piece over her mouth. The act stifled Vanessa's voice, leaving her with a sense of surrender to the unknown.

"I am taking the trash to the dumpster. You are going to sit here quietly until I get back. You don't want to know what happens to bad little girls."

Nila reached into her pocket and pulled out a small chain with a silver locket on it. Vanessa's eyes grew wide as Nila placed it in her hand.

"You know what this is and you know where it came from. How easy it was to find. Think about that while I am gone."

Vanessa looked down at the small piece of jewelry in her hand. It was a small heart-shaped locket that she and Abigail had both gotten for Christmas one year. A locket that held a picture of the two of them on one side and their parents on the other. Vanessa had put it in her jewelry box in her room the morning Nila kidnapped her. She usually wore it everywhere, but that morning she took it off because there was nowhere to hide it under the costume. Nila had been in her house.

The door closed with a thud, and the bolt clicked into place. Vanessa started to shake in fear. However, before it took over, she broke the back half of the locket off and tossed it toward the corner. The last piece of her forever attached to this place.

***

As each day slipped away, Abigail's hope gradually faded. Initially, the police suspected that Vanessa's disappearance was tied to their parents. Expecting a ransom demand, they anxiously awaited each phone call, their hearts leaping with anticipation. In those initial days, they clung to one another, not wanting to be separated even for a moment. Abigail's parents presented a united front, seamlessly complementing each other, working in perfect harmony like a well-oiled machine. They meticulously made lists, placed phone calls, gathered photographs, crafted statements, and even held a press conference, desperately pleading for the safe return of their youngest daughter.

However, deep down, Abigail sensed that there would be no ransom demand. Something felt awry, but she couldn't quite put her finger on it. She replayed that fateful day in her mind over and over, searching for any detail that could explain this unsettling feeling. The detectives questioned her relentlessly, dissecting every aspect of the drive to the ballet studio that morning.

They probed her about the conversations, the people present, and Vanessa's demeanor. They delved into the moment Abigail arrived to pick up her sister, scrutinizing every word exchanged with Mrs. Blanchard, questioning the state of the door, and investigating whether they were alone. And then, the crushing blow came: why hadn't Abigail called her parents to confirm who was picking up her sister? Why did she simply depart for shopping without verifying if it was a customary arrangement?

In the days that followed, the interrogations took a more intimate turn, shifting from a collective family experience to personal one-on-one sessions. Abigail found herself bombarded with inquiries about her parents' relationship, their daily routines, and even their not-so-perfect habits. But then came the probing questions about the frequency of arguments between Abigail and Vanessa, whether they ever escalated into violence, and if resentment ever simmered between the sisters. It was all becoming too much for Abigail to bear. It felt as if her family was being put on trial for a crime they weren't even aware of committing.

As the night fell, Abigail became burdened by the weight of unspoken regrets, lingering what-ifs, and haunting maybes. The gravity of it all threatened to suffocate her. Sleep became an elusive luxury she couldn't afford. The relentless pressure and strain had taken their toll on her, to the point where she hadn't even realized that Christmas had arrived until the city detective's unexpected call.

Puzzled, Abigail couldn't fathom why a detective from a different jurisdiction would want to speak with her. Her father, however, assured her that this detective could be trusted, offering a glimmer of reassurance in the midst of uncertainty.

"Just be truthful, Abbs. That's all any of us can do," her father's words echoed in her ears, urging her to face the impending conversation with unwavering honesty.

Abigail anxiously sat in her bedroom, her attention fixated on the ongoing conversation between her parents and the detective. She strained her ears, hoping to catch a whisper of her name drifting through the open door. As she perched on her bed, her gaze wandered to the faint outline of Vanessa's room across the hallway. Her mother had kept the door shut tight ever since the police had departed, treating it with an almost reverent care, as if preserving the pristine space of an adult rather than that of an ordinary eleven-year-old. Vanessa had always been different in that way, possessing an uncanny wisdom beyond her years and an almost obsessive compulsion for cleanliness.

Suddenly, the sound of footsteps echoed up the stairs, jolting Abigail out of her thoughts. She braced herself for the sight of her parents, their faces stained with tears. Instead, a woman dressed in khaki pants, a polo shirt, and a windbreaker appeared in her doorway. Exhaustion etched into her features, yet emanating a warmth and compassion that were hard to miss. Abigail's eyes were immediately drawn to the bulge near the woman's hip, concealed under her jacket, revealing her as the detective who had come to investigate.

"Hi Abigail, I'm Detective Morris. Your mom and dad mentioned it would be alright if we had a chat up here. Is that alright with you?"

Detective Morris projected kindness, her eyes sharp and observant, gauging Abigail's every response and movement. There was a genuine openness and understanding in her demeanor, something Abigail desperately craved in this unsettling time.

"That is okay if you don't mind sitting on the bed. Sorry, it isn't made. That was more of my sister..."

Abigail let the words trail off as she caught the tears threatening to spring up again. The detective sat next to her, quietly but not uncomfortably, more like she was giving Abigail time to collect herself.

"I can only imagine the thoughts going through your mind. I have never had this happen to me, but I have worked a lot of these cases, worked with a lot of siblings. I promise, whatever you are thinking, feeling, you aren't the first. I can't say that it is natural, but I can tell you, in my experience, it is a common thing. I am not officially working on your sister's case; I am here more in a consultant slash friend of your parents' way."

The detective took out a notepad and a pen. She flipped through the small pad until she found a blank page, then carefully folded one end up before turning to the next blank page.

"I'm not sure what information I can give you that I haven't already been asked a hundred times. If I had any information I thought could help, I would be shouting it from the roof. I've gone over the day so many times, trying to figure out what I missed."

"So, something feels off to you too? You don't think this has anything to do with who your parents are, do you? Let's start there."

"Too? You think this is something other than a kidnapping?"

"You said you have been trying to figure out what it is you missed, not if you missed something. That tells me something feels off to you. That is your gut talking to you. We just have to work past the guilt to help you figure out what it's saying."

"What makes you think I feel guilty about anything?"

"No need to get defensive, I didn't mean it as an accusation. I know you fought that morning; I know you were the last in the family to see or talk to Vanessa. I know you just missed picking her up. That would weigh on anyone, let alone a sixteen-year-old big sister."

Restless, Abigail rose from her seat and began pacing the room. Each step she took was an attempt to jog her memory, to grasp onto the elusive details that slipped through her fingers. She could sense that something had unsettled her, but the exact moment eluded her grasp.

As Detective Morris attentively scribbled notes, Abigail retraced her steps, recounting every detail she could muster. She confessed her anger when Mrs. Blanchard had casually mentioned that Vanessa had already been picked up. Lost in her own self-pity, Abigail hadn't even considered reaching out to anyone. It wasn't until her father's consecutive phone calls that she realized something was terribly wrong.

"Think back to the car ride, try to remember if you were drinking anything. What music was playing? Did you and Vanessa talk about anything?"

"I had my water bottle, and there was Christmas music on the local radio station. I left it on because Nessy loves that stuff, and I felt bad for not helping her do her makeup."

"What made you feel bad about it?"

"She was so excited to have the lead in the ballet. The entire reason she had to go in was for the final fitting and to have her photograph taken for the recital brochure. Nessy found out last minute that the lead had to drop out, and she was taking her place. The brochures were to be handed out to everyone at the Christmas festival last night, with her picture on the front. I remember looking at her and thinking she didn't do that bad of a job with her makeup, but I probably could have done better if I hadn't been so wrapped up in myself and so angry for her going through my stuff without asking."

"Now think about when you were looking at your sister. What did she have on? How was her hair and makeup?"

"Her hair was pulled into a tight bun on top of her head. She was wearing light pink blush on her cheeks and eyes. She had tried to put on mascara but missed the bottom lashes. She was wearing a white shirt with flowers or something on it, sweatpants, and a matching zip-up sweatshirt, with white tennis shoes. Oh, and the stupid silver necklace with a silver locket. She never takes it off..."

"What? What are you remembering?

"The weird feeling. I got it again when I was describing her. It's something about the way she looked. And she wasn't wearing the locket that day because of the costume and pictures. But I have one exactly like it in my jewelry box. My parents gave us matching ones when we were younger. One side of the locket has a picture of the two of us, and the other has a picture of our parents. It looks like this. What the hell?"

"What? What is it?"

"The locket isn't here. I haven't touched it in years, so it should be right here. I know it was here last week because I saw it when I was looking for a picture for a collage for my mom. That is weird."

"Did anyone else know you had this box or what was in it?"

"No. It's just an old cigar box that was my grandpa's. I just keep little things in it. Just sentimental stuff. Vanessa didn't like going near it because she said she could still smell nasty cigar smells. Besides, she didn't even know it was under this stuff. I will grab hers; she wasn't wearing it that day, so it should be in her room."

A few minutes later, Abigail came back into the room, holding a silver chain and locket. Her face was as white as a ghost. Detective Morris jumped up to grab her, scared that she was about to pass out.

"It was the make-up. It was wrong," Abigail said.

"Well, you said she didn't have much experience," Detective Morris replied.

"No, I mean her make-up is what has been bothering me."

Abigail reached into her purse and pulled out the folded-up brochure Mrs. Blanchard had given her at the studio. She carefully unfolded it and handed it to Detective Morris, revealing Vanessa's perfectly posed face on the cover.

"The make-up is different. Look at her eyes and lips. The mascara is fixed, she has on two colors of shadow, and a dark lip stain. I don't have anything like that. That is not how she looked when I dropped her off. And this is my chain and locket in her jewelry case. See how long the chain is? Her's is much shorter. And look, the clasp on mine is broken, so the locket doesn't stay shut."

Abigail dangled the necklace out for the detective. This time, it was Detective Morris who turned into a ghost.

| 12 |

CHAPTER 12

HARRIS, JANUARY 2022

Harris found himself navigating through the weekend and into the following week in a daze. The night training had thrown his sleep schedule off balance, leaving him in a perpetual state of restlessness. The events of that haunting night on the strip played on a loop in his dreams, as vivid as a scene from a gripping TV drama. Images of May's battered face and bruised body lingered in his mind even when he was awake, a constant reminder of the fear she had masked with a facade of control. May's distress was palpable, a mix of anxiety for her future and the very real threat to her life.

During the journey back to their temporary abode that evening, Harris remained silent, lost in his thoughts. His usual quiet demeanor made his lack of words inconspicuous, especially with the other guys in the car in varying states of intoxication. Pop and Slim had dozed off not long into the ride, their snores blending with the hum of the road beneath the tires. Ace and Buck, their speech slightly slurred, kept up their lively conversation from earlier, inadvertently leaving Harris to grapple with his inner turmoil, memories, and sense of culpability.

It wasn't until that Sunday when they had decided to cook dinner at the house, when Harris had stepped outside to do a perimeter check, that he realized one detail from the night hadn't gone unnoticed. Pop had been leaning against the side of the house, waiting for Harris to be out of ear shot of the group.

"You wanna talk about it?"

It wasn't a question as much as a request. Harris not completely focused had been thrown off by Pop. Not exactly sure what he was talking about at first. He gave him a quizzical look, showing his confusion.

"You haven't sat still for two minutes since Friday night. I assume it has something to do with your constant pacing last night and where your shirt ended up."

Something in Harris' eyes must have changed before he could conceal it because Pop was now standing toe to toe with him, his gaze staring into Harris' soul. Harris had never been good at keeping anything from Pop, or Hawk for that matter. If Pop was asking, he and Hawk had already talked. The two of them held conversations with just their eyes. Harris couldn't lie, but he honestly didn't know what to say. He wasn't sure why he was still so worked up. Why he couldn't just let it go. He did the right thing and did his best by May; the rest was up to her. This wasn't what they were here for and keeping a low profile was important. Unwanted attention would put the entire team at risk. He knew that.

"So why can't I let it go?" Harris heard himself asking at the end of his recount of that evening.

"You did what you could. These women get raped, beaten and sold, some before they are ten years old. You and I know better than most that the world is full of monsters. Monsters that exist to carry out the most horrific acts. She is lucky you showed up. You gave her a fighting chance. Sometimes that is all that you can do."

Harris knew Pop was right but his words made him anxious. Pop handed him a beer and he took a swig of it gratefully. Harris had a purpose here; he had a team and a mission that needed his attention. He needed to focus.

"Yeah, I better check to make sure we have everything for tomorrow. We have to switch out our gear for night ops." Harris started to walk away, turning back to add, "Hawk's been talking to you I suspect. I will be fine, thanks for the talk, Pop."

"You got it Doc. Hawk just worries about you."

Harris walked away half laughing. That was Pop's way of letting him know he was looking out for Harris too. Pop and Hawk had quickly become the male figures he desperately missed in his life. His own father had worked a lot, his mother too. Somewhere in his teens, they quite making excuses for not being around. Leaving Harris to fend for himself. He would be surprised if they knew when he was home or out most nights.

It was a crisp Wednesday evening, and as the sun dipped below the horizon, the group wrapped up their training session. Amid the clatter of gear being packed away, the team slowly made their way towards the neatly lined rows of vehicles stationed near the training grounds. Despite the reassuring words from Pop and the ever-watchful presence of Hawk, Harris found himself unable to shake off the memory of May and the unsettling events of that fateful night. The incident played on a loop in his mind, each scenario leading to darker outcomes for May after his departure. Harris couldn't help but envision her broken and discarded, her piercing screams echoing in his ears as she suffered for his actions. To add to his turmoil, haunting whispers from his past seemed to murmur his name in the gentle evening breeze.

The journey back home passed without incident, allowing Harris a moment of reprieve. Swiftly sneaking in a shower before the hot water dwindled, he absentmindedly brushed his teeth in the misty bathroom, his towel snugly wrapped around his waist. Lost in his thoughts, he inadvertently left his clothes behind and made his way down the hallway towards his room. The familiar sounds of Pop and Phantom sharing tales of yore to an engrossed Buck mingled with the clatter of dishes as Ace and Slim engaged in a playful scuffle over chores. Despite craving a moment of solitude, Harris' hopes were dashed as he stepped into his modest room, only to find himself face to face with Hawk.

"Ehhh, somebody has been working out," Hawk remarked with a whistle.

The smirk on his face and childish laughter not quite reaching his eyes. Harris knew it was time for a world-famous Hawk talk. They had talked about so much over the years Harris had been on the team. Hawk was a straight shooter but not quite as jaded as Pop. There was still some joy left behind Hawk's eyes they joked. Harris realized how awkward the silence had become. Hawk standing by the bed, Harris standing just inside the door, wearing only a towel.

Harris gave a half-hearted chuckle and closed the door behind him. He reached for his clothes stacked on a side chair. It didn't even phase him that the other man was in the room, he had been showering and dressing in crowded rooms since basic training.

"So, what do I owe the pleasure of your company this evening?"

Harris had thrown on a pair of shorts and shirt and was making his way to the bed. Hawk beat him to it, throwing himself in the middle then rolling on his side to face Harris. Hawk propped his head with one hand while patting the bed next to him with the other.

"Come on pumpkin, lets cuddle and chat about the future." Another round of laughter erupting from Hawk as he sat up, propping a pillow behind him.

"Pumpkin? You getting soft on me?" Harris quipped as he sat on the other side of the bed, reaching for a pillow.

"You haven't been yourself. I'm sure the incident in town last weekend got into that thick head of yours. What is nagging at you?"

Harris was prepared for a lecture, for smack upside the head, something about screwing his head on tight. This? This he was not prepared for. He took a deep breath, closing his eyes for a second, collecting his thoughts. Harris didn't need to think about what was nagging him, just needed to gather the nerve to say it aloud. Harris opened his eyes and looked directly into Hawk's, his tone flat and his face like stone.

"I need to find May. I need to go back and see she is okay."

The eyes staring back at him didn't falter, they held no judgement, just concern and above all, understanding.

***

It was surprisingly easy to convince the guys to embark on another trip to the strip, and even easier to plant the seed in their minds that it was their idea. The atmosphere was filled with anticipation and joy as laughter reverberated through the house in preparation for the hour-long journey. There was an unspoken agreement when Harris volunteered to be the designated driver once again, adding a touch of reluctance to his offer for good measure. Meanwhile, Ace and Buck engaged in a playful banter about which club housed the most stunning girls.

As the group readied themselves for the night ahead, everything appeared to be business as usual, just a bunch of friends gearing up for a night of letting loose. However, Harris couldn't shake off the slight guilt he felt, knowing that he and Pop were the only two privy to the hidden agenda of this adventure. They had crafted a plan to discreetly split up, just like they had done in the past. Once the guys were out of sight, Harris and Pop would set off on a leisurely stroll. While Harris had no clue which club May was working at, he had a distinctive outfit in mind to look out for. Their mission involved locating the club, entering it, and discreetly observing the surroundings. Harris had a strong hunch that May wouldn't be visible upfront or serving customers, but she would be there if she was indeed alive.

The original plan was simple: a quick check to ensure she was safe and breathing, no interaction, and then they would leave. It was too risky to get involved any further. Closure was all he sought, with secrecy paramount. This mission was to remain unknown to anyone else. After this night, whether he found May or not, Harris could finally move on, knowing he had done his best.

As they approached the vehicle, Pop settled in his usual co-pilot seat, while Harris headed for the driver's seat. To his surprise, someone was already seated there. Hawk and Pop's expressions left no room for argument. Harris reluctantly took a seat behind Hawk, feeling the weight of suspicion or perhaps his own guilt. Sensing the tension, Hawk lightened the mood with his signature goofball antics.

"Welcome aboard mates, this is your Captain speaking. I am Hawk the magnificent and next to me is my first and only mate, Pop. We will be providing you with nonstop transportation from point A to point B and back. I can't promise you the normal smooth ride you accustomed to with your former Captain Doc, but management has decided the stick up his ass has become lodged so far up there that his wee brain is getting splinters. He is under strict orders to get inebriated and laid tonight so I will be taking over. Please ensure to keep all limbs and family jewels stowed inside the vehicle at all times as Captain Hawk only provides wild rides."

Excitement filled the air with laughter and cheers erupting as the group embarked on their journey. Harris was greeted with encouraging pats on the shoulders, along with playful remarks like "about time" and "are you sure you remember how to use that thing?" Any lingering suspicion or tension Harris had sensed earlier had dissipated, replaced by an atmosphere of ease and heightened anticipation. As the car journey began, Harris leaned back, envisioning the night ahead, letting the chatter and banter fade into the background.

The drive seemed to pass by in a flash, thanks to Hawk's speedy driving and Harris' meticulous mental preparations for every possible scenario. Before he knew it, they had arrived, and Pop was delivering his customary "don't fuck up" pep talk. As soon as Pop finished speaking, the group spilled out of the car, heading towards the bright lights just as they had done a week before. They naturally split into their familiar groups, with Hawk embracing the younger teammates around the shoulders. Harris had expected to stick close to Hawk and Pop, but perhaps Hawk's presence was intended to keep the others engaged.

Taking a leisurely stroll, Harris and Pop made a pit stop at a sports bar, fully embracing their roles as tourists. About an hour into their time on the strip, they began their quest to find May in January.

As they strolled past the vibrant clubs, their eyes discreetly darted towards the alluring girls outside, careful not to attract too much attention. Harris had briefed Pop on the distinctive outfit, ensuring they both knew what to look for. After approximately fifteen minutes of searching, they came across the venue. It wasn't a dingy dive bar, nor was it a flashy, overcrowded hotspot. It managed to strike the perfect balance, standing out while blending in seamlessly—truly a master of camouflage in the bustling nightlife scene.

A small queue had formed outside, and they effortlessly merged in with the eager crowd. Pop slyly pulled out his phone, capturing a casual selfie of the duo. The snapshot seemed innocuous, a typical tourist move, carefully orchestrated not to raise suspicion from the vigilant bouncers. It wasn't just a memento of the night; it was a detailed record of the girls, the entrance, the venue's name, the imposing bouncers outside, perfectly timed to catch a glimpse inside. This picture would serve as insurance, swiftly shared with Hawk in case things took an unexpected turn.

It took roughly thirty minutes to reach the entrance, where they were greeted by a bouncer exuding the charm of a horror movie villain. Despite their lighthearted demeanor and slightly slurred speech, feigned for added effect, the bouncer inspected their IDs meticulously, shining a light over them and then their faces. Though the second pass of an additional device, obviously scanning the cards might have raised alarms for some, the details on the IDs were meticulously crafted, belonging to fictitious personas—a middle-level executive at a reputable marketing firm and a commercial contractor from New York City on vacation in Thailand. Each team member had a carefully curated set of alternate identities, designed to sail through security and background checks, with social media profiles maintained, deactivated, and reactivated as the situation demanded.

Harris' eyes took a moment to acclimate to the club's dimly lit interior as he followed Pop towards the bustling bar. They decided against snagging a table, knowing May wouldn't be mingling on the floor with her current disheveled state. As they waited for their drinks, they surveyed the club's layout, strategizing how to stay under the radar while keeping an eye on the staff. Pop's keen eye identified a prime spot just outside the impromptu dance floor—a perfect vantage point.

With drinks in hand, they weaved through the lively crowd before settling in. Amidst the thumping beats reverberating from the speakers, conversation was futile. Harris had already spotted five cameras, primarily focused on the exits, bar, dance floor, and the hallway leading to the restrooms—areas they had evaded so far. It was time to observe the eclectic mix of club-goers, hoping to catch a glimpse of their elusive target.

Two hours had slipped by without a trace of excitement. Eager to shake off the sense of being creeps lurking in the shadows, they sought out a new vantage point. The night was wearing on, the crowd swelling with each passing moment. The air buzzed with laughter and the clinking of glasses as people overindulged in drinks, while vigilant bouncers made their rounds.

Hawk's reassuring text about the kids enjoying themselves at camp provided a moment of respite, but the urgency to make a move lingered. As tables turned over and the atmosphere grew more charged, the girls circulated with the rhythm of the night. The elusive May remained out of sight, adding to the tension.

Taking a chance, they claimed a somewhat neglected table in a secluded corner, disregarding its unkempt state. A waitress appeared, all youthful charm and flirtation, ready to take their orders. Harris found himself momentarily lost in thought, pondering May's own struggles amid the harsh realities of flirting for tips and engaging in sordid encounters for money. The image of their waitress, her innocence juxtaposed against the seedy underbelly of the night, left a bitter taste in his mouth.

Barely acknowledging the girl meticulously wiping the table, Harris swirled his drink lazily. His gaze followed the mist of disinfectant settling over the surface, revealing a faint scent of lemon and stale water. A quick wipe with a grimy rag left him observing not the stains on the cloth, but the haunting scars encircling the cleaner's wrists and the fading bruises on her delicate forearms, the coloration seeming to be from a week prior.

With a conscious effort, Harris tore his eyes away from the girl's small hand to meet her gaze. Her face, concealed under layers of heavy makeup, held a defiant edge that even the most generous application of mascara couldn't mask. In a deliberate move, he carelessly dropped his phone onto the table, causing his drink to wobble precariously. As he instinctively reached out to prevent a spill, he nudged the glass away from himself.

The sudden commotion caught the attention of Pop, who glanced over, then shifted his focus to the startled girl. Harris, now on his feet, hastily gathered his phone, offering profuse apologies in his best southern drawl, hoping to dispel the tension that hung in the air.

The girl's eyes darted to his instantly. Harris asked her for more rags still apologizing. Then he looked at Pop and said, "Man, I told you January was my unlucky month, we should have waited until May to take a vacation."

"You are just as much a klutz in May as any other month. I think you've had one too many my friend. Maybe we should head out?"

"You're probably right. I've made enough work for this nice lady. We should probably go before I land on my face."

Harris looked into May's still swollen eyes and apologized, "I truly am sorry for any trouble I caused. I'm just glad I didn't make a bigger mess. My friend and I will be getting along now. Have a good night."

The apology rang with sincerity, a silent acknowledgment passing between them, transcending the mere spill of a drink. May's tense frame relaxed slightly as comprehension overtook the fear in her eyes. For a fleeting moment, she savored the flicker of kindness before being enveloped once more in shadows.

Unaware of the curious onlookers now fixated on them, they suddenly found themselves under the scrutiny of two imposing bouncers closing in, accompanied by a sharply dressed man advancing in their direction. A hasty departure at this juncture would undoubtedly raise suspicions not just for May but also for themselves, their identities already logged upon entry. They had no choice but to think on their feet and embrace the art of improvisation.

"Is there a problem? Did something happen here?" the man asked with a slight accent that was far from local.

"No sir, I'm afraid my friend here just had one too many of your fine drinks and spilled a little. I am afraid he may have gotten a little on your employee and was just apologizing."

"Nonsense, my customers never drink too much and they never apologize to the staff. This one is just new, but she should know to be more graceful, yes?"

May nodded, her gaze locked on the floor, the stiffness back in her shoulders. Her hands curling the dirty rag in a knot around her hands. Harris felt the heat coming up his neck seeing her so frightened at his expense once again.

Pop was attempting to settle things down, explaining it was on them and that they would settle their bill and go. They didn't want any trouble for anyone, throwing in that they would pay for any damage they may have caused. Explaining they were just on vacation, blowing off steam after a long year of hustling.

This seemed to draw interest in the man, "You have come to the right place to loosen up my friends. No need to hurry off. As long as you are spending money, you are causing no problems. Stay, look around, see if there is something you might like, maybe not on the menu."

Pop started to decline but Harris knew he had to make this right. He pulled out the large sum of money he had brought in case they ran into trouble, pulling out enough to cover the tab, making sure the man saw he had enough for anything not on the menu.

"This should cover the bill. We planned on catching a show a few doors down. We heard it is something to see." Harris added a wink and wry grin.

"No need to go anywhere to see beauty. Just look around. You see something that you like, and you can make your own show."

"What if I like this one?" Harris nodded at May.

"This one is not show material, a little rough around the edges."

"Well, I guess my luck is changing because rough is exactly my type." Harris stated, licking his lips while flipping money through his fingers and keeping eye contact with the man.

"A man that knows what he wants. Pay the bar tax and you have thirty minutes. Any longer and I come to collect my property and the tax goes up, a price that can't be paid in money."

"I'll have her back in twenty with a smile on her face."

Harris flung the wad of cash at Pop, a silent display of dominance, then gestured towards the bar, asserting his authority. He wanted the anyone watching to think he was in charge. In response, Pop returned with a poker chip, hurling it back at Harris with a disapproving glare. It was evident that only one of them would walk away with May, leaving the other on their own until the other's return.

As they exited the bar, Harris and May navigated through the crowd, Harris confidently displaying his chip to the bouncer. Following May to the place where it all began, Harris seized the moment when they were finally alone and abandoned his tipsy facade, turning to face her.

Although her back was turned towards him, Harris sensed no fear in May's demeanor. Instead, he detected a familiar emotion in her posture—disappointment.

"Are you okay? I mean did they buy the story?"

May turned around; her fingers paused midway down unbuttoning her shirt. Anger and hurt in filling her eyes.

"Are you joking now? You save me one day just to come and buy me another? Is this fun for you?"

"What? No. May stop. I don't want to sleep with you. I just thought he was suspicious and this would help. I knew they wouldn't have you on the floor so you probably are making any money. I was trying to help. I figured we could sit her for fifteen minutes and then I would take you back. I swear. I only came to make sure you were okay. That..."

"That you didn't get me killed?"

"Yes, exactly that. I felt guilty, I had to know you were as okay as you could be."

"A tourist who feels guilty. That is a first. A tourist who talks like a salesman and thinks like a wiseman."

"I guess we are both more than we appear. May, I swear I just wanted to help."

May sat down on the floor, pulling her knees to her chest. Harris sat down across from her. They just sat in silence for a bit. May seemed lost inside herself.

"I was twelve when they took me from my family. I don't even know if they are okay. The people who took me from my village told me they just wanted to help too."

Harris sucked in a breath. A pain stabbing at his heart. A pain he hadn't felt in a long time. He felt the guilt tightening in his chest, sucking the air from his lungs, his vision going blurry behind the welling tears. He looked away, pulling himself back to this moment. Leaving the past, focusing on May.

"You really were trying to help. Why? Why do care?"

Harris pulled out his wallet, he took out a small worn photograph and a paper that had been folded and unfolded so much it was starting to tear at the creases. He tossed them at May who picked them up and gazed at the photograph.

"She is beautiful. Who is she?" May asked while gently grazing the picture with her thumb.

"Someone who I was supposed to protect. Someone who trusted me. Someone who is gone because I failed." Harris could hear his voice shaking.

May looked at him with sadness in her eyes. She unfolded the paper and looked at the photocopy picture.

"And this?"

"That is what she would look like if she had been able to grow up."

There was a hollowness in his tone now. One May understood. May looked at the other side of the paper. She blinked several times then squinted. Her hands began to shake as the paper slipped from her grip, floating to the floor.

"What is this? Who are you? What do you want?"

"What are you talking about. May, what's wrong? It's okay, we still have a few minutes before we have to head back."

"Why do you have that? How do you know her?"

"Who? What are you talking about? I told you, it just a computer program that ages a picture. It is what the girl in the photograph would look like if she had lived."

May reached for the paper again. Looking it over, flipping it back and forth, the looking at the picture next to it.

"Not her, this one."

Harris realized there were two aged pictures on that paper. May wasn't talking about the girl in the picture, but another girl that haunts him.

"That is another aged simulation of another girl who died. A year after the other girl, a few miles away from the first. They were about the same age. They got lost walking home in Florida many years ago. They were never found, they died."

"No! No, you can't be here. I have to go; you need to leave here and not come back. I can't talk to you."

"May, what is going on? If you know something about Daphne or Vanessa you have to tell me!"

"I don't know any Daphne or Vanessa. I have to go, don't follow me."

May was scrambling off the floor as Harris pleaded with her.

"May, please! They were just little girls."

May was almost to the door. Harris was stuck, unable to make his body move.

"I don't know Daphne or Vanessa; I know Natasha and Viktoria. They have been here with their uncle from Russia, and the little boy. I don't know anything else; I swear to you. You have to leave me alone. I can't be involved with this. I am sorry."

Then May was just gone. Faded into the shadows. The world was closing in around him. Harris couldn't breathe, his vision was going dark, sweat pouring down his neck, his heart pounding so hard he could feel it throbbing all over.

Harris wasn't sure how long he had been standing there. The next thing he remembered was a voice telling him to breath in his nose and out his mouth, then cold water splashing in his face. Reality started coming back in waves. It was a minute or two before he recognized the figure as Hawk. Of course he had been shadowing him. Then it all came flooding back. Harris bent down and picked up the paper and picture. He started toward the door.

"Let her go Doc. You got what you came for. She's alive, we can't say the same for Pop if we don't get that chip back and make sure she went to the club from here."

"She is alive. They are both alive."

"Good, I would hate to think that was a ghost that just flew past me. May, right?"

"Yes. I mean no."

"That wasn't May?"

"That was May. I mean they are alive."

Harris pressed the paper with images of Daphne and Vanessa in Hawks chest. Both of them staring, jaws open and eyes wide.

"May saw them. She knows who they are with."

| 13 |

CHAPTER 13

DAPNE, FALL 2010

Daphne flipped the visor down and adjusted the vanity mirror from the passenger seat so she could see her face in the dim light. Nila was driving and had some music on that she said reminded her of "home", wherever that was. Daphne knew this little field trip was taking them about forty minutes outside of the small town they had recently moved to. She had her script memorized and was applying the make-up needed for her part. Light pink blush, nude eyeshadow, no mascara and just a hint of lip gloss. Her hair was secured in two perfect braids on each side of her head. Nila had chosen a pleated plaid skirt in pale shades of blue, green and white, a white Oxford collared shirt, socks with lace and black shoes that buckled over the top. All though, Daphne had just celebrated her thirteenth birthday, she looked like she was ten all over again. That was the point tonight, she was a very young, very obedient Viktoria.

Satisfied with her make-up, the now 'Viktoria", flipped the visor up and stared out the window. The city was different but the scenery was the same. Highways littered with endless taillights, seedy motels with flickering lights, truck stops and dinners lining the exits. When Daphne first graduated from "photoshoots" and home movies, to what Nila called adventures, she had become Viktoria. The first time she knew she was going out she was mixed with all kinds of emotion. Thoughts of how she would escape flooded her mind and adrenaline flooded her body. Daphne had envisioned herself kicking and screaming, making a scene, drawing as much attention to herself as possible. Someone would notice, someone would ask questions, someone would help.

Those thoughts were extinguished with a crushing blow when Nila had come into her room as Daphne dressed. Nila had brushed her hair and asked how she was feeling, even bringing her some 7-up to help ease her nerves. Nila had seemed so nice, concerned even. Nila had told Daphne how nervous and scared she had been the first time Uncle had taken her on an adventure. Daphne had thought she saw a tear form in Nila's eye. Then Daphne saw the small envelope Nila had placed in Daphne's lap. With shaking hands, Daphne had opened the cream-colored envelope, it had a smell that was so familiar, almost welcoming. Daphne pulled out the small paper and photograph from inside. It was a ticket to her brother's homecoming dance and photograph of him standing with her mother. Then it made sense, the smell was her mother's perfume. Nila had been in their house again; she had been in her parent's room. That is when Daphne knew there would be no escape plan.

***

It was quiet in the dark room. Too quiet if there was such a thing. Occasionally her heart would slow and the pounding in her ears would recede. That is when all she could hear was the ticking of the small bedside clock in the dingy hotel room. This wasn't her first time in this room and the shadowy figure just outside the cracked door wasn't a stranger to her either. She was dropped off an hour and twenty-two minutes ago. That meant she had thirty-eight more minutes until Nila would knock on the door. The man knew he had thirty more minutes until she had to be ready.

Nila was punctual if nothing else. Every man that did business through Nila, understood her threats weren't empty and the coldness behind her eyes was earned. Nila scared everyone, the clients, the girls, people who walked by her. Only the man she answered to, the one who gave Nila reason to be so cruel, made her bat an eye.

She was hypnotized by the methodical tick of the clock, eyes growing heavy with sleep. She didn't hear the man close the door as he returned from his cigarette break. She could feel her mind easing into the darkness, tension releasing from her body. Somewhere in the back of her mind, a voice was telling her to wake up, to move, to talk. The clock was too calming, overtaking her.

It was just too easy to let the dark take over. To let her mind wonder to a world where she had been happy, a time when life was easy and safe. She knew she shouldn't give in to the temptation, somewhere beyond the calm, was reality begging her to open her eyes. Begging her to fake the enthusiasm that would get her through the next half hour. She was just so tired.

Tired of pretending, of feigning interest, of dressing up, of being someone she wasn't.

Life was cruel that way. One day the happiest times of your life are playing dress up. Pretending to be a movie star, or a model, the next big thing in stardom. Trying your hardest to be seen, to get all the attention. The next moment, all those things are what your nightmares are made of. The only thing you want is to become invisible, to crawl up inside yourself and hide from the world. Suddenly being the least popular is what you crave. To be able to hide your body from prying eyes and the rough hands of strangers.

"Tick, tick, tick." Then a searing pain on her left buttocks, a sizzle drowning out the tick of the clock. There was just pain and the smell of burnt skin, then a soft cry before the man closed it off with a hand over her mouth. She could smell the thick smell of tobacco, tasting smoke as she tried to open her mouth for air.

Her first instinct was to buck and kick, to bite a chunk out of the first chubby digit to slip past her lips. She had to fight every natural urge, willing herself to keep her mouth shut and allow her body to be moved at will. Anything else would leave her with more than small burn. If it wasn't inflicted here and now, she would pay later. This was a fact; one she believed to her core.

This wasn't the first man to treat her like trash to be thrown out. Hell, it wasn't even the first time this man treated her like nothing more than a possession, bought and paid for, to with as he pleased. Nothing more than an object without feelings or rights. Here, she had meaning, she had no life worth caring for. Here she wasn't anyone's daughter, or sister, or friend. Here she wasn't even human. Here the neighborhood mutt was treated with more care.

"Good girls don't fall asleep on me. You bored girl? You must be bored. Need a little reminder of what you're here for. It ain't sleep darlin'."

His chubby hand engulfed her small face. His knee parted her legs and he was inside her again. She knew better than to cry, than to say anything. She was thankful she didn't have to see his face this time, that she could close her eyes and let her mind take her somewhere else until it was over. Her dark hair hung forward, covering her face. A face she barely recognized.

Just like that, Daphne let her mind take her back home. Home to her mom and dad. Back to her bedroom, across the hall from Shane. A place where she was a child getting ready for school. A place far from the hotel room where, at twelve years old, she had to be a woman.

***

Shane sat in Detective Morris' unmarked sedan, staring at the unremarkable building situated behind a small church in a town only minutes from his own. The last two years had not been his best. His family was falling apart, he couldn't remember the last time he picked up a bat and to frank, his grades were less than stellar.

His parents had taken him to family therapy, to a therapist of his own. There had been tutors, summer school and groups for teens experiencing grief. None of it helped when everyone had stopped looking for Daphne. They even had a memorial service for her earlier this year when one of her shoes had been found with what the lab had identified as animal blood.

The general consensus was she had gotten lost walking home in the storm. Disoriented by the driving rain and washed-out paths. With the new finding, the obvious conclusion was that she had been defenseless against a black bear that had been frequently sighted in the area, even though the only things ever found were one shoe and the small tassel she had carried to support Shane's team.

The news had been devastating, but it seemed less so than the unknown, than the constant directionless searches. Leads had come in hard and fast in the weeks following her disappearance. People had called from all over the country saying they had seen his sister. Daphne had been seen in a diner having breakfast with a family in Texas, shopping with friends at a mall in Michigan, even camping with a church group in Tennessee. All during the same time periods usually. Then there were the psychics who felt Daphne was surrounded by water, taken in by a cult, and even part of a circus crew.

Detective Morris had kept Daphne in the headlines by calling in favors with newspapers and constant pleas from the family during the numerous press conferences. There had been coordinated searches, fundraisers, interviews, and visuals. Numerous people who had known Shane's mother through her job as a social worker had started social media pages. His father's small OBGYN practice was well known enough to get some support from the community for some time. However, when the next big headline came along, Daphne was barely a tagline.

The turnout for the service had been quite large, especially for a young girl of only ten. There had been family, friends, co-workers, people from the town, officers that had worked the case, girls from cheer camp, and even guys from his baseball team. Pretty much the only people who weren't there were members of the media. None of the newspaper reports or television outlets that had camped on their lawn for weeks, that had called their home at all hours, followed his mom to the grocery store, or waited near the ballpark. A new story had caught their attention and the little girl they had demanded answers for was long forgotten.

Part of Shane was full of rage at the media. They had put his family through hell. Put every aspect of their lives on public view. Made accused without basis, harassed them all, gone through their trash for more than a month. Now, when it was time to put Daphne to piece, they wanted nothing to do with it. For them there was no scandal, no dirty laundry, no horrific headline. The other part of Shane didn't mind because they were all standing there mourning an empty coffin. Daphne wasn't even there, why should they be.

The only news coverage of the memorial had been the full-page obituary Shane's parents had bought. It featured the cheer photo taken the day of Daphne's disappearance that took up half the page. The rest was a synopsis of her short life on earth, followed by all those who lived on, missing her every day. It had been printed right there in the local paper, "survived by her older brother Shane." It was sickening to see, to read, to know in his heart that the words were printed because of him. The only thing that had stayed consistent was Shane's guilt.

Shane didn't know if he was comforted by dimmed limelight or saddened. He knew, no matter what happened that day, it was his fault. He knew it and his parents thought it. After the service his parents seemed to put on the charade of moving on, of healing. Behind the scenes though, it was tense conversations behind closed doors, sharp silence when Shane entered the room, and empty conversation for his sake.

No matter what happened that day, Shane knew in his heart, Daphne was still out there. He didn't buy for one minute that Daphne was the victim of weather and nature. He knew she was out there and no one was looking. No one but him. That is why it was so hard to focus on anything. He was angry, frustrated, no one was listened, no one cared. His sister was out there, somewhere, with someone, and she needed help. Shane knew it, he would tell anyone who would listen. The problem was, everyone had quit listening, writing him off as a grief-stricken kid refusing to see reality. The truth was, Shane made secrete that he felt it was everyone else who refused to see reality. To see what was right in front of them.

That is what brought him to this building, on this day, in Detective Morris' car. She was the only one that seemed to listen. To not dismiss him because he was "just a kid." She may not agree, but she didn't shut him down, she didn't think he was crazy. That was the reason Shane had agreed to attend this meeting. It was another peer grief support group, like many others he had been to. Detective Morris encouraged him to try this one specifically. She said there was someone who had been attending this group for a few months that she felt he would find interesting. Whatever that meant.

"It's time kid. I'll wait here for you. If it isn't your gig, I will be here. I'm just asking that you give it an honest try. You don't even have to talk. Just promise you will listen. Can you do that for me?"

Shane got out of the car, looking at the building, then back at the car. The look on the detective's face was open and hopeful. She had been there for Shane from day one and never left his side. This was the last place he wanted to be on a Friday evening, but how could he say no.

"It's the least I can do, I guess. I'll see you in a bit."

It took fifteen minutes for introductions before the man who had introduced himself as Mr. Petrov, a counselor at a local private school, to ask if anyone wanted to share. At first there was the usual awkward silence, the shuffling of chairs, the sound of jackets zipping and unzipping. Then a voice filled the room. It was soft but firm, confident.

Shane looked for the source, turning in his seat, shifting his gaze left and right. Finally, he found her, a brunette with porcelain skin, about his age, sitting near the back. It wasn't her looks or voice that had him entranced, it was her words.

Suddenly the insistence on this group, on this meeting, made sense. He knew why he needed to be here today. For the first time in two years, Shane felt himself letting hope back in. He found a home in this group, in her.

Listening to this girl talk calmed Shane's heart. He felt tension leave his body with each word. He knew he would be back, as many times as could.

***

"Why are you so quiet? Not that you are a chatty one, but tonight, this is different"

Daphne wasn't in the mood for Nila. The burn on her ass was rubbing against the tight denim of her skirt. She was tired and the man had been more rough than usual. She felt ill, tired and homesick. All things Nila considered childish nonsense. Daphne just wanted to stare out the window and let her mind take her back to her home, to her family.

"Whatever it is, you better get over it soon. Your night doesn't end for two more hours. Better to cheer up and make the best of it little one."

"I know. It's not my first day you know. That creep put his cigarette out on my ass. Do you have any cream in here?

"Shit happens. It could be worse. Look in the glove box."

Daphne shuffled through the array of receipts, random papers, condoms, wet wipes, and body sprays until she found a small tube of some type of ointment. She shifted in her seat, hiked her skirt and applied some cream to the burn.

As cold as Nila was, Daphne knew Nila had been through all the same things. She experienced the same abuse, fear, and had the scars to prove it. Her icy exterior was just another scar. Nila had been doing this for far longer than Daphne. Even if Nila wouldn't admit it, Daphne knew Nila had dreams of her own.

They had talked over the years; Nila had a family of her own once too. Long ago, even though their memory had faded, she knew this was not her life. Nila had someone to answer to, just as the small group of girls answered to Nila. Someone that Nila feared so much that she did not dare try to run.

Daphne had no doubts Nila was capable of carrying out all the promises she made to them if they tried anything against the rules. She knew Nila had been in her home long before their meeting, that Nila could find her way into anyone's life and destroy it. Daphne had to protect her family, even if this was her life now. Nila had described, not only her home in great detail, but also what would happen to her mother, father and Shane if she ever fell out of line.

Just the memory of those conversations brought a chill deep in Daphne's bones. She drew her jacket tighter around her thin body. Quickly she replaced any fear she had behind her eyes, with the same emptiness Nila carried before turning back in her seat. There wasn't anyway Daphne was going to let anyone see that there was any part of her that remained human. Humans were weak, they could be manipulated and used. So that part of Daphne would stay hidden from the world, locked away in vault only assessable to her.

| 14 |

CHAPTER 14

CRANE, JANUARY 2022

It was earlier than usual when the coffee pot started to drip, and Murch was letting me know his disdain for being waken before the alarm. I threw on my running clothes while I waited for that first cup of caffeine. Murch looked up, letting out a slight groan when the lights came on. Sleep had come around 2 am. Racing thoughts waking me every hour. I am tired but there is so much to get done today and I have no idea where to start. At 4:30, I had finally given in and pulled myself out of bed.

I downed the coffee while tying my favorite running shoes. Murch realized I wasn't going back to bed and made his way to the front door where his lead was kept. I gave him a loving nuzzle as he slipped into his lead and it was secured.

"I know buddy, I didn't get much sleep either. We need this though."

I took my time, making my way through the neighborhood I had grown to love. Keeping a steady pace while I let my thoughts organize themselves into a mental to-do list. My talk with Angel a few days before had given me a heaviness in my stomach. It also gave me a feeling that I was on the right track, a sense of momentum that I had to keep following his case. I couldn't shake the feeling that this was important, that I needed to see this through.

The day after, I had created new usernames in more online chat groups. My search for any handle having to do with tattoos was a bust but I wasn't giving in. While I waited for some unknown person to take the bait, I had started reviewing all the images the Digital Unit had gotten from Angel's electronics. It proved to be a daunting task, not just because of the sheer number of files, but because I had no fucking clue what I was looking for. I just knew it would pop out when I saw it. I had started making spreadsheets of different outfits, ages, ethnicities and forums. I wasn't even a quarter of the way through and Digital was still finding more files.

I needed something that would get me back into Angel's house. I had to find the missing device. Something inside told me the answers I needed were there, even if I didn't even know what the questions were. This man was haunting my dreams, replacing faces and appearing in the nightmares I've struggled with most of my life. Today I needed to find a connection to get a new warrant. I needed to get the images cataloged. I had to keep active in the chats and hope for the best. There was so much to do and new cases were piling up. I need something substantial soon or this was going to have to be tabled.

I loved everyone in my unit and they deserved my attention and time. No one had complained yet, but the strain of long hours was starting to show in more faces than mine. It was only a matter of time before Sarge saw my dropping stats because Angel was consuming so much. I wanted to be there for them all before I got called into the principal's office. Not to mention the several emails from the DA asking for my finalized case packet.

Just as my legs started to feel like sludge, I saw my street up ahead. Even Murch was panting and whining. I checked my watch, just over thirty minutes since I left. I had set out for and easy jog to clear my head but ended up with a seven-minute mile average. I guess my mind had distracted me enough to push harder than I had intended.

Back in the seclusion of my home, I grabbed another caffeine cup and picked out my outfit for the day. Murch was already back in bed, not a worry in his mind as he snored lightly. He hadn't even touched his food. I watched him sleep while the water was heating up. I don't have a single memory of the last few years that didn't include my furry partner in crime. He really had a way of keeping me grounded. I made a mental note to schedule a little park time for him this weekend.

I was out the door and heading to work before 6 am. An idea hit me as I drew closer to my office and I made a detour towards the local coffee shop. I ordered donuts, bagels and coffee for the team and steered back toward the office. I had made great time leaving so early, skipping the usual traffic, and we all needed a little treat.

***

I was entranced by multiply monitors running several programs at once. I didn't even notice someone had turned on the lights, let alone come through the door. It was the smell of freshly brewed coffee that gave Adam's arrival away. I turned towards his desk just as he handed me a fresh cup. I slid off my headphones, giving my eyes a break from continuous scrolling.

"Hey, didn't hear you come in. There are bagels and donuts in the break room. I even got your "a little of this and more of that" latte's."

Adams was out the door before I could say any more. He returned with his caffeinated mixture in one hand and several treats balanced on a paper towel. I watched him navigate his way to his desk, hands and mouth full. I checked the clock, shit already 8. Guilt flashed over me and I quickly signed into the ICAC data base to check the new cases. Just over 80 new files stared back at me. I meant to have them organized before anyone came.

The guilt must have been written all over my face because Adam's was staring at me, waiting for me to meet his gaze.

"How long have you been here? You look like you slept here."

"A few hours. Time completely got away with me. I'm sorry, my intention was to have the log cleared and organized before anyone got here. I'm on it now, promise."

"Promise? What is this, kindergarten? You look like shit Crane."

I gave him a sheepish smile. I fucked up. I knew it and he knew it. If I didn't get through these cases, the whole team would know it. I took a quick break to go in the bathroom to freshen up. When I came back, my partner was already sorting through the data base files.

"Let me finish that. I owe you that, at a bare minimum."

I started clicking through files and closing out dead end or irrelevant leads, assigning real CSAM cases between us. Giving myself a few extra. When I finished, the new cases had been dwindled down to twenty-six, assigning myself fifteen and the rest to my partner. I quickly scanned emails and checked my voicemail. By nine the office had filled and I had checked a few things from my to-do list and added a few more.

"Damn Crane, you look like shit"

The Cpl had made his was to his desk, a stack of napkins and donuts next to his keyboard.

"Seriously? Did the two of you get together and find the insult of the day? I quipped as I gave a little grin.

"I just call it like I see it, and shit is how I see it," Vickers quipped.

"Just what a gal wants to hear," I said, flicking a rubber band his way.

I was reviewing a fresh file sent over from the Digital Forensic Team. It wasn't marked CSAM, but "Urgent Per Your Request". Slightly confused I opened the file, noting it was a 90 second video labeled .Mp4. The attached report concluded the video had been retrieved from Angel's cellular phone and also recorded on the same device. I watched the video in its entirety. It was exactly as Angel had described when I talked to him at the jail. In the video, Angel held a photograph of a young girl, possibly eleven to thirteen years old, wearing a cheerleader uniform. It was just a still photograph of a youthful girl posing for a photo. With his other hand, Angel was rubbing his penis vigorously. I knew it was him by the tattoo on his finger.

I forgot I had emailed the digital team to immediately notify me if they retrieved any files like this after my interview. I'm glad I had, otherwise this file would have been discarded. As disturbing as it is, there is nothing illegal about it. It did however corroborate Angel's account of how he received the CSAM. I sent digital another email, thanking them for the file and asking if there was any way to find out where the video had been uploaded to or where the photograph of the girl came from.

On my fifth review of the video, two things stood out to me. Neither of which had to do with Angel's appendage. First, the device he was holding with the picture of the girl. What was it? Where was it? The girl wasn't a family member so why did Angel have a framed photo of her? I knew the video was taken in his home from the small fragments of the couch and coffee table in the background. A framed photograph of a little girl would stand out. Second, the cheerleading uniform the girl was wearing. The photograph didn't seem to an old photograph, yet the uniform itself seemed worn and definitely not her size. Why have your child's photo taken in a dingy, ill-fitting uniform? The uniform itself didn't seem generic either. Not something you would pick up a costume store. Maybe handmade? Or passed down?

The one thing I was hoping to give me answers was giving a headache and more questions. I closed my eyes and willed myself to focus on one question, one detail at a time. Focusing on the little girl. Her stance, the look on her face, her body language. I had no experience with cheerleading so this was taking me nowhere. I was just about to give up when the image of my partners screensaver came through my mind. I was seeing his desk, his computer, the images of his sweet family, then the photographs next to his desk.

"Holy shit! Adams, come here." My eyes shot to the picture frame shuffling through one nauseatingly cute picture after another.

"What ya got?" Adams answered rolling his chair over to mine.

I explained how I had asked digital to send me any videos or images similar to the ones Angel said he sent to get CSAM. I cued up the video and had Adams watch it several times. Then asked for his thoughts.

"The obvious being Angel likes kids because he has a micro penis."

"Seriously, look at what he's holding in the other hand. Focus on the picture itself."

Adams ran the video again, stopping, rewinding, and replaying a few times.

"That's a digital frame! It has a USB for photos. If it is anything like mine you can set it to randomly rotate or to stay on one picture. If it was set to one picture, we would have walked right past it!" Adams was getting it now.

"Exactly what I was thinking. Now look at the girl, focus on just her. Your girls did cheerleading for that church program, right?"

Adams was already replaying the video. He stopped it thirty-four seconds in, a clean shot of the girl without Angel making a debut. Adams made a screenshot, then clipped it so it was just the girl, enlarging it a little before printing it.

It seemed like hours went by before Adams lifted his eyes from the printout. I could tell he had latched on to something though. We had worked to many hours in close quarters not to be able to read each other's minds, body language and eyes.

"This pose is generic. It isn't something you would do for a cheer picture. The girl is really uncomfortable in it. She obviously hasn't posed this way before. She's not a cheerleader. And if she looks uncomfortable, she didn't choose to dress up as one either. Then there is the uniform. I think it is an actual uniform. Those colors and the mascot are really familiar for some reason."

This is why Adams and I work so well together. We are both detail oriented. I take a puzzle and put all the edges together and he fills in the rest. It made sense now. I wasn't looking at a photograph of an innocent young girl having her cheer picture taken, I was looking at victim. Victims could be tracked.

"I'll see if we can clean that image up a bit. Maybe we can get a hit on the uniform."

"And I will get a new warrant for that digital frame," I said already pulling up the template.

| 15 |

CHAPTER 15

VANESSA, SPRING 2016

Natasha loved the beach, feeling the warmth of the sun on her face, the breeze tangle through her hair and the soft sand under her feet. Most of all she loved hearing the giggling boys only feet away, mesmerized by whatever shinny object they discovered in their bucket. Krathing Lai Beach was beautiful. The beaches spread as far as you could see in either direction, the food was amazing, and the people were warm. This place was special for many reasons, it was a gift.

It had been two years since she was last here. So much has changed. It was in Pattaya, just south of here, where she first learned she was pregnant. After all the years of being beaten, raped, mentally and physically tortured, Natasha didn't think anything could break the walls she had built. Standing in the bathroom, staring at the second pregnancy test, willing it to change to negative, she felt herself breaking into tiny pieces. The last bit of hope and faith left her body, leaving her cold inside and out.

The year before Natasha became pregnant, Viktoria had gotten pregnant. Nila had told them she too had been pregnant years before. Nila had become very ill and Uncle had to take her to a clinic. Uncle had terminated the pregnancy and things between them had changed forever. The clinic he took Nila too was an off the books, ask no questions type. The environment was barely ideal for the ill, let alone surgery. Nila ended up with an infection that nearly took her life and left her sterile.

Natasha remembered Viktoria being torn. On one hand not wanting that monster's child growing inside her, but also not wanting her life to end on a dirty back ally surgery table.

When Uncle found out Viktoria was pregnant with his child, he wasn't angry like he was when Nila had been pregnant. Instead, he was elated, even taking special care of her throughout the pregnancy. The best doctors, clean hospitals, vitamins. He was a proud father. We were all surprised.

Then the baby came, a sweet chubby boy. Viktoria was instantly in love with her son. It had been a hard labor, with only the mid wife. Natasha had held her hand and whispered, "You can do this Daphne."

Rarely did they use those names. They had long ago decided that they did not want the vile, disgusting world they were now a part of to tarnish their old lives as Daphne and Vanessa. So, they chose to become Viktoria and Natasha full time, not just when meeting men. Every now and then, when there was a happy moment, they would seal it by using their real names.

After Viktoria had spent six weeks with her son, whom she had named Christopher, Uncle had taken him away. Uncle had her sign the birth certificate as Viktoria Broska and given her son the name Nikolai Broska. Viktoria was heartbroken. Uncle used her son to make her do what he wanted. She would do what he needed her to do in exchange for a week with her son every few months. Now it made sense. The child was just one more bargaining chip. They didn't know where their children were when they weren't with them. That was cruelest form of torture they had to endure.

After Nikolai came, Uncle came to Natasha's room almost nightly. The rapes were violent and with one purpose, to impregnate her. Once she found out she was pregnant the attacks stopped. She too was given the best care. Uncle was once again a proud papa.

Natasha's labor was the same as Victoria's, the same midwife. This time Viktoria whispering, "You can do this Vanessa." Natasha never bothered to think of a name for her son. There had been no point. Uncle would name him whatever he wanted before whisking him away. Natasha had tried to be distant. She had tried to remember how he was conceived. But one look at her boy and she just melted. She would do whatever it took to see him for that week every chance she got.

Natasha smiled as she watched Nikolai and Alexei chase the water as it receded back into the sea. She wished Viktoria could be with them too. Uncle never let them come together. Natasha was here with Uncle this week and next week Viktoria would make the trip with Nila. This was the safest way for them to travel. There had been a big arrest two years ago in Thailand involving an important Russian friend of Uncles. He said it was too dangerous for them to come here all together. Natasha wondered who it was dangerous for, them or Uncle?

Over the years girls had come and gone. It was usually a quick transaction. Nila would bring in a girl, or occasionally a boy, who fit a client's preference, a few photos were taken, maybe a video, then they were gone. Two weeks was the longest any of them had stayed. They moved around a lot, all over the country. The only time they left the US was to come here to Thailand. The only ones who traveled with Uncle to Thailand were Nila, Natasha and Viktoria. Sometimes, Uncle would return from a trip abroad with a child, but he never left with one.

As far as Natasha and Viktoria could understand, they were the only planned kidnappings. A lot of planning and time had gone into both their abductions. Other than Nila, they were also the only two Uncle kept. Why were the three of them so special

***

Abigail worked so hard to get to this day. She had finished her bachelor's degree in two years by taking dual enrollment classes in high school and a full course load during the summer terms. Finishing her Master's in a year and a half had burned her out. Then five months of the police academy finally brought her to this day. Abagail was being sworn in as a police officer at the city's police department. It was something she had dreamt of since she was sixteen, since Vanessa was taken from their lives.

Abigail never stopped looking for her sister. In college she used her role as the University's newspaper to keep Vanessa's name out there. She also had a memorial page on social media, organized fundraisers, talked on local radio shows and used any other outlet she could think of. Even if the rest of the world gave up, Abigail was still doing everything she could to find her sister. Not just Vanessa but her best friend's sister too. Shane's sister went missing eighteen miles away in the next town over, a year and a half before Vanessa. Both girls had went missing in similar circumstances but there was never enough evidence to link the cases.

Abigail met Shane at a peer grief support group recommended by Detective Morris. Detective Morris was the primary detective on Daphne's abduction and had consulted on Vanessa's case as a favor to Abagail's parents. Abigail, Shane and Detective Morris were the only three people who saw a connection in the abductions. If it wasn't for the two of them, Abigail didn't know how she would have survived the last seven years.

Meeting Shane helped Abigail find purpose again. The support group allowed her to express her guilt with people who understood. When she expressed her thoughts about feeling there was more to her sister's kidnapping, the therapist, Mr. Lensky, would say it was guilt trying to make sense of a senseless act. Shane was the only one who understood. Shane also felt something was off about his sister's disappearance. There were just too many inconsistencies, to many similarities with the cases.

The issue was, they occurred a year and a half apart in two different jurisdictions. Shane's sister, Daphne, was thought to have gotten lost in the woods during a rainstorm on her way home from cheer practice. This theory was solidified when one of her shoes was found deep in the wooded area far off the path with animal blood on it. Shane wasn't convinced though. They had found a charm that Daphne kept on her backpack in between to homes in a neighborhood to the north of theirs. It was close to a cut through off the path further up.

Abigail's sister, Vanessa, had been classified as an abduction. There were no clues as to where the abduction occurred. Mrs. Blanchard, Vanessa's ballet instructor, watched Vanessa Walk out with the rest of the class as usual, but never saw her after that. All the other girls were interviewed as well, none of them seeing who she left with either. There were no cameras in the area where Vanessa would wait to be picked up. The only thing they were sure of is that surveillance video showed Vanessa walked out of the studio with other students. Another camera from a neighboring business didn't show any other vehicles coming or going except the photographer who had been shooting at the studio and Abigail arriving. Wherever Vanessa went, it had to have been from the opposite direction where there were no cameras.

After Abigail told Detective Morris about the swapped charm necklaces, she had put out a press release with a photograph of the one Abigail had. Two months later, an apartment manager called in a tip.

A cleaning crew had found part of a charm with an engraving on the back and a picture on the front. Detective Morris identified it as half of the matching charm. The apartment was forty-five minutes outside of town and had been leased short term by a company with fraudulent documents. Not only did the company not exist, but none of the board members existed either. A canvas of the complex yielded nothing. No one remembered seeing anything two days prior let alone two months. After that everything went cold.

***

Abigail stood on the stage in her uniform, feeling proud. Her eyes searched the crowd, first landing on her mother, then Detective Morris who would swear her in, then the empty seat where her father should be. Abigail felt a tug at her heart, thinking about her father's funeral the year before. He suffered a stroke that took him quickly. His loss further devastating their already broken family. She hoped he was looking down, proud of all she accomplished.

Abigail continued to search the arena, looking for one more set of eyes. She had sent the invitation without expectation. She didn't even know where in the world he was. She hadn't seen him in years, not since she flew up to see him graduate boot camp. She knew it was a long shot that he would even receive the invitation let alone be able to make it to the ceremony. But she had hoped.

The ceremony was full of emotion. Abigail felt a sense of pride and duty she hadn't expected. For the first time in years, she knew this is what she was meant to be doing. Detective Morris had tears in her eyes when she stood in front of Abigail, reciting the oath that would become a staple in Abigails life. She smiled brightly when the crowd erupted in applause. Beaming with pride, her eyes fell on a figure standing in the rear of the auditorium, smiling as wide as she was. He had come, and all was perfect, almost.

| 16 |

CHAPTER 16

HARRIS, JANUARY 2022

In the two days since May ran off into the shadows of Pattaya, Shane replayed those last minutes of their conversation a hundred times. He wasn't sure if he was searching for something he missed, some whisper or glance he was too stunned to remember, or if he was replaying it to convince himself it really happened. For fifteen years he turned every stone, looked in every corner of the universe for some crumb of evidence Daphne was alive. Now, thousands of miles from home, during a chance in counter with a stranger, he had found not just a crumb but a whole fucking piece.

Shane remembered every second of that night with May. He could recite every word they spoke. For the life of him, he couldn't remember one minute of the rest of that night. It was as if his brain stopped computing after May disappeared into the darkness. There were blurs of faces, voices talking around him that he couldn't focus on. Every muscle in his body was both tense and numb at the same time. He had run into gunfire, crept through unknown territories, hunted people who wanted him dead, never once blinking an eye or missing a breath. Now he was in a tunnel. Lights flashing all around him, radios playing different tunes on different frequences. All he could focus on was May.

She had been so certain when she looked at the picture Shane carried with him everywhere. So absolute when she identified the women in the age enhanced photographed. There had been no hesitation, no second glances. May had been positive and she had been terrified. Her words had solidified what he had always known. Daphne was taken; someone took her. Vanessa had been taken too. Now he knew they were together. They were alive.

Shane was knocked out of his thoughts by a tightening in his chest. He had literally been knocked back to reality by Pop's boot to his armored chest. They were finishing up the days training, getting ready to head back to the rented house for the night. The group was still in full gear from the days training so the kick to the armor was more jolting than painful.

"Get your head in the game ass hat." Pop looked pissed as he growled a few inches from Shane's face.

"Sorry Pop. I'm doing my best."

"The fuck you are. I know this is just training, but you owe them and us a hundred and ten percent from sunup to sundown. I've seen your best and this shit ain't it."

Pop was right and Shane knew it. You perform how you practice. If he didn't give all he had here, he could get someone killed later. Shane got to his feet and popped his ACH on. He gave Pop a nod, acknowledging he knew he was in the wrong. Shane left the makeshift tent they were using as HQ and went looking for a way to be useful.

"The kid is going through it old man. He's doing better than I would be." Hawk murmured, as he watched Shane Walk toward the group waiting for instructions.

"Hell, he does better than most of us in our sleep. We have a mission and that comes first. It isn't going to get much better. I got word from the brass. I have to break the news to him tonight."

"They didn't bite?" Hawk asked shaking his head, spitting in the dirt.

"Did you think they would?"

***

Shane was mentally preparing himself for whatever lashing was coming his way. He knew he had let Pop down, hell he let them all down, himself included. There was a thickness in the air from the ride home through dinner. Pop and Hawk had been exchanging glances, as if having a secret conversation with their eyes. Shane understood their anger towards him and his lack of performance. He was ready to deal with the consequences.

Pop, Hawk and Phantom were in Shane's room when he returned from his shower. It was starting to feel more like an intervention and less like a shit talking. Shane had already gone over his apology and prepared himself for whatever punishment they handed down. What came next, he wasn't prepared for.

"Are you fucking serious? It's my sister!! May knows her, has seen her. Seen her here. Seen her with another missing American! That isn't enough? They want me to just forget a witness knows where my little sister is? To just, what? Walk away like she told me the sky was blue?" Shane could feel the anger rising inside him. He wondered if the guys could see his heart pounding against his chest.

Pop was the first to speak, "It's bullshit. I get it. What the hell did you think was going to happen? A prostitute whose name might be May, who I might add, you solicited, said she recognized two girls from an old AI enhanced photograph. Two girls she knew by different names.

And let's not forget, the witness this all hangs on, refuses to talk to anyone, especially you!"

Pop was right but this was all wrong. They had torn apart villages looking form men pictured on a deck of cards with flimsier intel than this. Shane had devoted everything to his country and now they wanted him to walk away from the only sliver of information about his sister in more than a decade. None of this felt okay.

"At the very best, we were looking at a humanitarian mission to aid the Thai government in rescuing trafficked women. If, and that is a big IF, they recognized there was a problem and asked for assistance." Hawk was standing now; he was speaking what everyone else had been thinking sense they forwarded the information up the chain.

"I get it. It was a long shot. Jesus Christ, it's my sister. We all know May isn't a prostitute. She isn't doing this by choice. You saw her. She was terrified. If my sister was here, and May recognized that picture, then she was here as an adult, not a child. That means someone has had her for fifteen years. If she was here, you all know what that means. You know what has been done to her, is being done to her! And I'm being told to just forget about it." Shane felt tears forming in his eyes, felt his body start shaking. "I let her down once, I can't do it again."

"I talked to one of the Thai military guys. I've trained with him before. I asked a few questions. Just basics, nothing specific. There is an NGO operating north of here that might be able to help. No promises. He's going to forward the little bit of info I gave him and ask some questions about any foreigners, specifically European or Americans. The guy will come through if he can. His sister was taken from their village when she was nine. He will try." Phantom was a living representation of six degrees of separation. If he says he knows a guy, he knows a guy.

"Christ Phantom, this isn't helping. We have four days left in country. What are thinking?" Pop looked like every vein in his forehead could blow at any minute.

"I'm thinking of my fucking daughter, of my sisters, that's what I'm thinking"

The guys left Shane to get himself together. If Thailand didn't have a human trafficking problem, then why did they have Nongovernment Organizations (NGO's) operating here? Shane grabbed his laptop out of his go bag. He needed to do some research of his own. First, he needed to get a hold of someone, maybe to only person who would understand what he was feeling.

***

Nila didn't like this. Something felt off, nothing specific but something that had the hairs on the back of her neck standing up. The feeling had been with her since she returned from the bar in Pattaya. One of the girls working the front had gone out with an American but never returned. The bouncers said a group of men had come in a few nights ago. May had waited on them and one had requested to pay her bar fee. May was on tables after an incident with another customer the week before, she wasn't supposed to go out. The man had insisted on her, flashing a roll of money.

The manager let her go. That problem was being dealt with. The man returned a short while later but May hasn't been seen since. The men haven't been back either. Nila had tried to review cameras but the group had somehow managed to avoid every angle. Even the scanned IDs were clean. Maybe too clean. This just felt wrong. That was a problem for the local crew. Nothing here could be traced to her or Uncle. May would be found, one way or another.

Nila shook away any tension she felt before entering the vacation home. Here, everything had to be normal. The boys were getting old enough to pick up on the littlest things. They rarely got to see their moms, and Nila would never admit it, but she loved watching them together. A chance to have children of her own was stolen from her. Not that she would ever bring a baby into these conditions.

In the beginning she was resentful of Nikolai and Alexei. Often, she would take that resentment out on their mothers, sending Viktoria and Natasha to the brutalist men. Now she saw that Uncle hadn't given them the boys as a gift, it was a form of torture. Torture he had spared her from. Now Nila held no resentment, she wished the boys could be with their mothers more often. They needed this time, especially as they got older. She could some of Uncle's traits in them. It was not something to take pride in. In reality, it frightened her.

| 17 |

CHAPTER 17

CRANE, JANUARY 2022

Crane plashed more cold water on her face, trying to calm her nerves. Her heart was still racing and the ground felt uneven beneath her feet. She inhaled deeply, counting to four, holding for four, releasing for four, a technique she had learned in counseling. Her hands trembled, her knuckles white, as she gripped the counter while trying to ground herself.

The last two days played on fast forward in her head. First finding the digital frame and USB at Angel's house. Then getting the downloads from the Digital Forensic Team. The images of young girls in various outfits, poses, lighting, seared into her brain. There were so many pictures, all innocent on their own, but together, in context with what they were used for, were overwhelming. The girl's ages ranged from eight to around thirteen. Most of the pictures were newer, maybe taken within the last two years, but there were several older pictures. Those Crane and Adams estimated to be anywhere from ten to eighteen years old.

There were more pictures of the same cheerleading uniform, worn by different girls. The same uneasy and frightened look on the young faces. However, there were a few of one girl, with a different background, that look more natural, and very familiar. Something about those particular pictures had Crane on edge. Every fiber in her said that photograph meant everything. She just couldn't see what.

Feeling a little less shaken, Crane grabbed some coffee from the breakroom and made her way back to her desk. Adams was working on new tips that Crane had been neglecting. Her partner was amazing. He understood she needed to see this through and had taken on more cases, giving her time to follow up on a few things. One of those things had been contacting the ICAC home office to inquire about any database that tracked photographs that did not fall under CSAM but were linked to CSAM cases. Photographs like the one hundred and sixty-four they recovered from Angel's USB.

Crane's ICAC contact had come through in a major way. Those photographs were cataloged and organized by age, gender, race, background, type and basically any other feature you could image. If an IP address was attached to a photograph, that was cataloged too. This is how they were able to link photographs and videos to "series" or collections of the same subject, in the hopes of identifying the victim. Crane had uploaded and sent them everything she late last night.

Adams had created a Crime Bulletin featuring the cheer uniform they discovered. The Crime Bulletin was distributed to all law enforcement and agencies that could have information relevant to assisting them in identifying the uniform. If they could figure out if the uniform belonged to a specific team, they would know what area it came from. Then they could search for contacts to track down who the girls wearing the uniform might be. Crane believed the uniform belonged to at least one of the girls pictured wearing it.

It was a waiting game at this point. Waiting for ICAC to finish cataloging those photographs and waiting for any information on the Crime Bulletin. Waiting to for someone to bite on any of the chat groups she had created over the last two weeks. Crane felt like her life had been put on hold, everything had just stopped all around her. A feeling she hadn't felt in thirteen years. Vanessa had been invading her thoughts and her dreams ever sense she arrested Angel. She didn't know why this case had brought her back to her sister's abduction. The cases were nothing alike, but her subconscious was tightening them together with each new development.

"Hey, I think we might have something on that bulletin. Someone from Homeland, said she'll only talk to you." Adams gestured toward the blinking light on my desk phone.

"Homeland Security? I thought you put your name on that?"

"I did. Said she needs to talk to "Abby" right away?"

Only her mother called her Abby but she certainly didn't work for Homeland Security. She had been Crane since college. Now her interest was piqued.

I pressed the blinking line and hoped for the best, "Crane."

"Abby, it's Morris."

"Detective Morris?"

"It's Agent Morris now. I work a joint task force with Homeland. Been here the last five years or so. Better gig than retirement."

"Well damn, what can I do for you Agent Morris?"

"I think it is more what we can do for each other. A Crime Bulletin came across my desk from someone at your agency. I don't know who the girl is, but I definitely know the uniform. It's an old one that was used by a community cheer camp in Brackton County."

"Brackton County? Wait a minute, how old are we talking?" Crane was already flicking back through the pictures, looking for the one that had been nagging at her.

"They started using that particular one in 2006 and changed it in 2009."

"What's your email? I need to show you something"

As soon as Agent Morris finished spelling out her email Crane attached the image, she thought was the original owner of the uniform. The one she felt was an actual cheer photo. She held her breath as her computer made the "swoooosh" sound, indicating the email was sent.

"This photograph was seized with other images in a current CSAM case. Tell me I am just seeing things."

"Oh my God. Abby. That is Daphne Harris. That is the picture that was taken the day she went missing. If that is the same uniform on the other girl, we got it all wrong."

"I can't believe I didn't recognize her. Something was nagging at me, but I should have known it was her. Agent Morris, there are several photos of girls wearing that uniform. Many photos of girls taken with that background. I already sent them to ICAC to be cataloged."

"Tell me who you are in contact with over there. Maybe I can grease the wheel a little bit. I will call you back when I have something."

Crane hung up the phone still in disbelief. She could feel tears burning the back of her eyes. She needed to do something, anything, to busy herself. She couldn't afford to lose it. Not now, not when after all these years she finally had something to grasp onto.

***

Crane, Adams and Cpl Vickers huddled in a circle. Vickers had been on the phone with the powers that be for twenty minutes and they had been breathing down his neck trying to hear more than one side of the conversation for fifteen of those minutes. So far, they were unsuccessful at hearing anything but had their toes rolled over three times, their heads smacked twice and now were getting long armed backward. Vickers was laying out a good case but he was repeating himself a lot. Any half decent detective knew his point was being bought.

Vickers finally hung up the phone and let out a long sigh. He took a long moment rubbing his face before turning toward his captive audience.

"Here's the deal. The Harris case is off the table. It is not and has never been ours. Not only do we have zero stakes in that game, but Crane you are way too close to be objective. You are to send Brackton County and Homeland Security any and ALL information we have acquired that can assist them with that investigation. You can continue to follow up any leads in the current Angel case as it pertains to his current charges. Do you understand that? You can work anything that will strengthen the current charges, nothing more." Vickers sounded stern but looked defeated.

"Are you serious? What about the other girls? We just pretend we didn't stumble on a collection of images taken in the same clothes at the same location? Images that are being used to obtain CSAM? And that is just what we know for sure."

"Crane, I get it. I really do. I tried. But we have no jurisdiction on this and you have a hundred other cases that we CAN work piling up. Don't think I haven't noticed your partner picking up your slack. People are working on it, let them do their job. And you start doing yours. Unless you want to see if your uniform still fits. Are we clear? Both of you?"

"We're clear," Adams mumbled as he wheeled himself back to his corner.

"Yea, loud and clear," I said with a little more attitude that I should have.

He was right and knew it. Adams was working his ass off to keep up with our case load while I chased ghosts. I had real victims right in front of me that I was neglecting. I trusted Agent Morris to follow through. The picture I had of Daphne was one we already knew was taken; one her family had already received from that day. There was no proof that uniform was hers. No other images had been found of her. The truth was I was angry at myself. I just took it out on the wrong people.

I closed out my open screens so I could focus on opening new tips that had been accruing over the last week. I was ready to open the ICAC database when I saw how many neglected emails I had. I started deleting the "reply all" and random emails to get down to a manageable number.

A few minutes in, I saw an email from an address I vaguely remembered. The subject line was simple but to the point: WE WERE RIGHT. I opened the email and felt the room start spinning.

Abbs,

Out of the country. Found someone who saw them. Recently. Together. We need

to talk, NOW.

Shane

| 18 |

CHAPTER 18

HARRIS, JANUARY 2022

Shane was exhausted. Not only was he putting every ounce of himself into the training tasked on him, but he was spending every free moment researching Thailand, human trafficking, laws and government. His body needed rest, his muscles were knotted and aching. It was his mind that couldn't be silenced. Even whiskey couldn't give him the release he needed. The once calm, focused and centered, SSgt crumbled into the now reckless and crazed stranger searching for ghosts in the wind.

Abby had replied to his email with just a phone number. She was still living close to home, giving them an eleven-hour time difference. Truthfully, that was only part of the reason he wasn't calling her. He had been worked up when he sent the email. Not that he wasn't still barely making it minute to minute. What would he say to her? How would it sound? Now that he replayed Pop's conversation back, all he really had was a needle in a stack of needles. A possible needle in a stack of needles. The small part of his brain that still hung on to logic knew he was seeing what he wanted to see, hearing what he needed to hear. His heart, that part of him he packed away behind cement walls, was screaming that he was close.

Logic had gotten Shane far in life. Numbers, facts, statistics, they were practical ideas backed by science and trusted trials. These were key elements that training scenarios, manuals and intel reports were made of. These things couldn't be skewed by emotions, didn't take feelings into account. They could be trusted. Gut instinct, those unexplainable seconds of knowing, when everything inside you is telling you to go against logic, that saved lives. Had saved his life more than once. Gut instinct couldn't be taught. It came from intuition, real experience and awareness. Right now, logic and gut instinct were at odds. Logic was telling him to let go; gut instinct was telling him to run into the fire.

Yesterday concluded the team's part in the joint training exercise. The better part of the morning had been spent cleaning gear and conducting sensitive items inventory. After lunch, Shane had completed the sensitive items check list, signing off that everything was accounted for. These items are things the military deems to be critical in nature due to schematics, intel, or mission related information that if obtained by the wrong people could be detrimental to national security. Not every item on the list is what you would think is a national secret, such as ammunition, night vision, or even radios. However, the last thing our government wants is a foreign government headlining that civilians were shot down with American bullets or our radio frequencies being used by cartels.

Someone will come behind me and re-inventory, double checking before adding the second signature. Then the gear boxes will be sealed before transport. When stateside, another inventory will be conducted, ensuring every last item down to the batteries are accounted for. It is tedious work, but necessary. Shane didn't mind doing it. It kept him from having to plaster on a fake smile and participate in meaningless conversations about what bar who was hitting up or what girl was lucky enough to get a call when we were home. Shane just didn't have it in him to care. If he was occupied with a task that required his full attention, he was thinking about Daphne

Shane thought about how selfish he was back then. Daphne was so proud to be his sister. She would paint her face with his little league colors and make up cheers for his games. Back then he had been embarrassed, even pretending not to know her. The last day he saw Daphne he had been so angry that he had to walk her home instead of getting pizza with his friends. He had taken his time packing his gear, even walking as slow as possible without walking backwards, just so she would have to wait. If he had just done what he was supposed to do. If he had been on time, Daphne would still be here. He could almost hear her voice, "Sh-aaanee, cheer up buttercup."

He would give anything to go back and do things different. To be a better brother. He wished he would have appreciated how much she loved him, looked up to him. He found out how much he needed her when it was too late to tell her. His biggest regret in life. The skeleton hidden in the darkest corner of his closet.

Shane skipped dinner to pack. They were heading back to the states tomorrow and he wanted to finish packing. He didn't have much to stow in his duffle so it was a quick process. A few pairs of jeans, a couple shirts, socks, his hygiene kit, shower shoes, four uniforms and boots.

With that out of the way, Shane powered up his laptop. He signed into his email. One from his mom, a couple of advertisements and another reply from Abby:

"Found this working a case here. A"

There was a .jpeg file attached to the email. Shane opened the file. Seconds later he was staring into a pair of eyes on a little girl that were an exact copy of his own. Everything around him faded away.

***

Shane stared at the image of Daphne, perfectly posed, her arms in a "V" high above her head, pom-poms mid shake, one leg in a high kick. A smile plastered from ear to ear on her ten-year-old, perfect little face. Her hair was perfect, her eyes were shining, she was perfect. Shane had seen this photograph many times before. It was taken the day Daphne went missing. The photographer had dropped them off days later. Daphne's coach had brought the pre-purchased photo package to the house, she had been sobbing when she handed them to Shane's mother.

A few headshots from that package had been used in news blasts in the following weeks. However, there had only been one of that pose, and 8"x10", that still hung framed in his parents living room. How had this photograph gotten out? And how the hell had it become part of one of Abby's investigations? Shane googled his sister's name, query any images that came up. This photo was nowhere he could see on an internet search. Confusion was setting in as he clicked photo after photo.

A rap on the door broke his concentration. He wasn't in the mood for company. When Shane didn't respond, he expected the intrusion to go away. Instead, Pop gave the door any pound before announcing himself, "Cover up, I'm coming in."

Shane tore away from the image he'd been staring at, willing to come to life, to speak to him. Pop's body language was stiff, his eyes heavy, but there was something else there, something contradicting the anger exuding around him. Shane and Pop shared a long history, they had been through battle, divorce, break-ups, endured loss like no other. Normally Shane could tell where a conversation was going just by the way Pop stood. But Shane wasn't firing on all cylinders and nothing was normal anymore.

Pop made it to Shane's bed in three heavy footed strides. Not his usual swagger, nothing about his movements showed the layer back mannerism Pop's was known for. Pop's aggravation only grew as he flung a folder at Shane with more force than needed. It was a brown folder fastened with a band. It wasn't thick, but it contained several papers of various sizes. There was a single sheet clipped to the outside. Shane barely had time to skim it before Pops tossed a pen, barely missing Shane's head.

"I know you have shit going on. Real shit. I get it. So, I'm going to make this short and simple. You're going to sign that without giving me any shit. You're going to pull your head out of your ass and make this shit right. You're going to be a God damn soldier again."

Pops was fuming and Shane was beyond confused. He looked back at the folder, really looking at the paper. It was a counseling form. A form that said Shane fucked something up. It would follow him in his unit but eventually would drop off. If he fixed whatever he did, it's possible it might disappear altogether. Otherwise, it would come up anytime he put in for schools, promotion or special missions. Shane knew his head had been fucked since his meeting with May. He tried searching through the blur of the last few days to find what he had done that lead to this point. Shane started reading over the fine print so to speak.

"Just fucking sign it. You were in charge of the first count. You put your John Hancock on the line accounting for everything. When Hawk did the final four items were weren't there. Do you hear me kid? Sensitive items, you said you touched aren't there! Lucky for you it isn't anything major. Probably at the training site. But you're responsible."

"Pop, I swear, everything was there. Every hole was filled. You know me. I don't make mistakes like that. It doesn't matter what's missing, this is serious shit."

"Damn right it is! Next transport out is in three days. Phantom is staying behind with you. The two of will backtrack to the training site tomorrow and do a thorough search. The rest of us leave in the morning. You best find the Uncle Sam's shit and be on that transport before this counseling turns into an official investigation son."

Before Shane could even respond, Pop grabbed the signed form and left the room, leaving the folder behind. Everything was falling apart. Shane could feel himself being swallowed by a force he couldn't see. The world was crumbling beneath him, his world was spinning out of control. Shane felt sick, physically ill.

Phantom came in the room and shut the door behind him. With one hand he picked up the folder, he placed the other on Shane's shoulder as if trying to ground him in place. "Just breathe brother."

"I swear everything was there when I closed the boxes. I've never messed up a check in my entire career."

"Calm down homie. We will find it. No worries"

"Easy for you to say, it's not your ass online. I didn't look to see what it was I supposedly lost."

Phantom grinned wide and picked up the small pack he had placed next to the bed. "If I had to guess." he said, dumping the bag onto the bed, "it would probably be these."

Shane looked down and saw two pair of Nods (military night vision goggles), a pair of headset radios, and an ABIS (automated biometric identification system). Basically, the bare minimum you might need for a recon mission. Now Shane was really confused.

"What the fuck man. I'm in serious shit over this."

"No, what you are is giving Pops plausible deniability. Did you even open the file?"

Shane grabbed the file, removing the band to reveal several papers, a map, a couple of pictures and two ferry tickets. He recognized a few things from the research he conducted on his own. The map was of a place called Phuket Island. Phuket Island is one of Thailand's more famous beaches located in the Andaman Sea. Recently, a large Russian population had started settling in the area. In 2014 several members of the Russian mafia, to including the leader of a prominent gang, were arrested in Thailand. Since then, several bars in Pattaya had come under new ownership, Russian ownership. The papers provided intel that girls, weapons, money and drugs were being funneled through some of these establishments and into condos on Phuket Island. A few people had stated that on more than one occasion, a group consisting of three females, an older male and two boys, travel to the island at different times. The females frequented two of the clubs on the strip. They were not regulars and were never seen all together. It was possible the girls could be those the Americans were asking about.

"Your source came through"

"Sure did. They have enough to worry about with the boarder problems to the South and North. Even the local bad guys don't want these Russian pricks around. If your sister has been here, that island is where we will find answers."

Shane filled Phantom in on the email Abby sent. He explained how he knew Abby and that the other girl could possibly be her sister. Shane and Phantom spent the next few hours looking over what they had and cross referencing it with the research Shane had done. By the time it was early morning in the states, they had formulated a plan.

"I think we can work with this. Time to make a call."

| 19 |

CHAPTER 19

CRANE, JANUARY 2022

Crane spent the rest of the day forcing herself to think only about the new cases she was filtering through. Several hours after her tantrum with Vickers, Crane managed to review fifty-three new tips of those she closed thirty-four as not being CSAM, transferred another eight that were not in her jurisdiction, and sent out preservation requests to the remaining eleven various internet providers and pertinent accounts. Now she was organizing her open cases on her shared spreadsheet, color coding case numbers to represent their investigation stage. This allowed any member on the team to open the file, search any case number and see where the case was by highlighted color. It was a simple system and when they were able to stay on top of it, worked well.

Staying on top of it was the problem. Herself and Adams were the only two detectives that worked Internet Crimes Against Children. At any given time, each were responsible for around one hundred cases each. All in different stages. Vickers was the Cpl and would take cases when someone was on vacation, in a class, in trial, or if a big case broke. Vickers also took on the responsibility of writing grants, meeting with brass, coordinating search and arrest warrants. He was pretty much their buffer from the world so they could do their jobs. Occasionally they would get a bright-eyed officer with dreams of becoming a detective temporarily assigned to them to gain experience. The temporary assignment lasted anywhere from two weeks to a month. However, with shortages in patrol, and more sexy units like gangs, the felony unit, tac, or narcotics, they didn't get many takers these days. Truth is, this job wasn't for everyone, it wasn't for anyone for that matter.

For the last few months Vickers had managed to get them their own dedicated analyst. Macy was a godsend. She was working on her master's at the local university and was a wiz at anything electronic. Vickers was a part time professor, teaching an evening course in criminology. Macy was his TA last semester and between the two of them, they were able to get a grant from The Center for Missing and Exploited Children that covered her salary. Thanks to that grant, Macy belonged to the ICAC task force solely.

Before closing out the spreadsheet, Crane clicked on the case number for Angel's case. Hovering over the drop down at the end of the row for a few seconds, then reluctantly clicking on "cleared by arrest", instantly highlighting the row yellow. It was heartbreaking, there was so much more that could be done here. I could feel it in my gut, in my heart. But facts were facts and the facts were, I had taken the case as far as my powers would allow me. Agent Morris and Brockton SO could work the other angles. I wasn't abandoning it, just handing it off to the right people. Then why did I feel so awful?

"Vickers needs to see you, he's in the break room," Adams said as he headed out the door.

I turned off my monitors and pulled the door shut behind me. Our offices had to be secured when unoccupied due to the sensitive nature of our work. It could be traumatizing to others if they say some of the graphic things we worked on. As if it wasn't traumatizing to us.

Vickers was sitting at a small round table in the corner of the break room. It was a shared space with several other investigative units so it was quite spacious as break rooms go. Oddly it was also empty other than the two of them. The clock on the wall showed it was quarter after four, late in our day but not so late that everyone would be gone. I suddenly had the feeling I was meeting with the principle.

"Have a seat," Vickers pointed to the chair positioned across from him.

"Listen boss, I'm sorry about earlier, I was out of line. I'm just—"

"I know, I'm sure I would feel the same way if I was in your shoes."

"Then why do I feel like I'm about to get a week of detention?"

"Listen kid, you have been hard at it for weeks. Great work on the Angel case. I saw the spreadsheet and your caught up. You have been working hard and fast for a while. Take some time off, you have plenty on the books."

"Boss, I'm good, really. I just had a moment."

"Crane, I'm not asking. I'm telling you either, officially. I'm strongly suggesting you take a week before I have to tell you"

I wasn't getting detention; I was getting benched. Suddenly everything started crushing in around me. The weight of the last week was squeezing me from the inside, taking my breath away. I could feel the warmth creeping up my neck and into my cheeks. My eyes were burning and wet with tears. My shoulders started to shake.

"Crane, this isn't me punishing you. This is me helping you. You are great at what you do, you have the best instincts I've seen in a long time. Use them. Take a week and work this out. We have you here."

Vickers got up and squeezed her shoulder, standing there for a minute before walking out. Crane took a few moments to steady herself. She took a few deep breaths and wiped her eyes on the sleeves of her sweater. When she was ready, she stood up, pushing in her chair. That's when she noticed the folder on Vickers seat. She picked it up, a sticky note on the outside read "good luck kid." Crane opened the file and flipped through the contents. It was a copy of her sister's old case file, a printout of the ICAC catalog results, and some other information she would have to dive into later. Vickers had a heart of gold.

***

Crane had been pacing across her living room for hours. Trying to piece together the information from the file and from her own research. She had taken Murch for a quick run when she got home, showered and fed them both. Now, glass of wine in hand and papers pinned to the wall, she was trying to put together a puzzle without all the pieces. Murch was laying on the couch, his favorite tennis ball under his chin. It was Tuesday, with the weekend she had five days off to work through all of this.

Murch perked up and let out a whine. "What is it boy?"

As if answering there was a knock at her door. Who the hell was coming at this time of night, better yet, who was knocking on her door at all?

Crane grabbed her weapon off the side table and walked softly to the front door. She seldom had visitors, when she did, they were expected. She looked through the peep hole and saw her partner standing awkwardly on her front step. Crane unlocked the bolt and sheepishly hid her weapon behind her back before opening door.

"Adams, uh... nice to see you?"

"Are you going to invite me in before you shoot me?" Adams gestured toward my gun hand. The man knew me too well.

"Sorry, I wasn't expecting company. Come in. What are you doing here?"

Murch jumped down and excitedly greeted our unexpected guest. He loved Adams and was happy for the extra belly rubs. Adams made his way into the living room. He studied my push pin puzzle wall in between "who's a good boy" and "am I your favorite?" His eyes followed the timeline I was trying to construct.

I had pictures of Daphne Harris in her cheer uniform from 2007, followed by other photographs of girls in the same outfit, some I was able to date from the ICAC catalog at 2008, 2010 and 2012. In between were pictures of the same girls in other outfits, including Daphne. There had also been thumbnails of videos that she didn't have access to from home. One of the thumbnails, she swore was Vanessa. Included in the catalog were photographs of other girls, appearing as early as 2000. The first in the series dated 1998. That child was photographed and videoed over the years up to 2003. She seemed to be the first and a favorite.

"So, this is where the magic happens?" Adams was mesmerized.

"This is where I drive myself crazy trying to make sense of a bunch of puzzle pieces that I'm not sure go to the same puzzle."

"Maybe this will help. When I left today, I went to see a friend and got you this. It's a copy of the Daphne Harris file. My friend owed me a favor so there's no paper trail. I'm pretty sure Vickers used connections to get you Vanessa's so nothing leads back to you."

"So, you knew he was going to tell me to take some time off?"

"Him and I talked. We knew you weren't going to drop this. We knew you couldn't. We figured this was the best way to let you do what you had to do under the radar. Crane, if it was my sister, or one of my girls, nothing would stop me. Just be smart. Use your resources. We are here for you, but there are people who aren't."

"I don't care about my job but you guys can't jeopardize yours-"

Cranes phone interrupted her mid-sentence. First a late-night visitor now a caller? I'm not sure I like this newfound popularity. She didn't recognize the number or the prefix and was about to send it to voicemail but remembered she had left a few messages.

"Crane"

"Abs?"

"Shane?"

"Yea, sorry about the time"

"No, it's okay. I'm glad you called. I have so much to tell you."

"Same here. I have you on speaker with my friend Phantom. we need to talk."

"Ok, I'm putting you on speaker with my partner, Adams, we have info for you."

Introductions were made and a quick catch up of pleasantries. Phantom broke the small talk first.

"I'm sure it's been a while, and everyone is fantastic, but we are in a bit of a time crunch here."

Shane explained that he was in Thailand on a training exercise. He told Crane about his chance encounter with May and her identifying the age enhanced pictures of Vanessa and Daphne as frequent travels called Viktoria and Natasha. Shane explained that they traveled with an older man, another female and a child. He went over the intelligence they had so far from the NGO in Thailand.

Crane told them her discovery of the photographs, the information on the catalog profile ICAC had provided, and the information she got from the interview with Angel. Crane said she had been contacted by now Agent Morris who was working some leads and she was still waiting on some IP information.

"So where does this leave us?" Shane asked, sounding completely overwhelmed.

"Basically, with a lot of information to piece together on two continents. And I've been sidelined. I can't investigate this officially. My boss gave me time off for all my hard work recently. I have very little rope to work with."

"I'm in the same boat. I sent the information up my chain and basically was told we have nothing. A prostitute that saw an AI picture and called them by different names. I'm only still in the country because a few inventory items were temporarily misplaced. I have three days."

"So, what now?" Phantom asked.

There was a deafening silence as we all weighed our options. We had no starting, ending or middle.

Adams spoke first, "Shane, you said May recognized the age enhanced pictures? If they are the same ones Crane has, they are the from last year's workup. We use their photos in a training class, that class was last year so they are fairly new."

"Yea, so? She ran off when she saw them. She won't talk anymore. The girl was terrified. It's too risky to go showing those pictures around here. I don't even know which one she knew as Viktoria and which one was Natasha."

"Ok, but if she had seen them recently enough to identify them, they must have passports. Those photographs are good enough to run through facial recognition. And we have first names to narrow down parameters." Adams was on to something.

"How do we do that when none of us are supposed to be working on this?" I asked.

"Didn't you say some lady you both know is working this as an agent with Homeland Security?"

"Phantom I don't know you, but God, I love you"

"I get that a lot from the ladies. The intel my guy here worked up has a lot of Russian ties, so have her run American, Russian, Bosnian, Belarus. Work those names with different spellings, Victoria, Viktoria, Vyktora. Natasha, Natsha, Natacha. Cross reference any hits with another woman, older man or children with the same travel pattern or last name when you get one."

"Gotcha, I'll work with Agent Morris on my end and keep trying to find the website that was being used. What is your plan?"

"We have good information on Phuket Island. We will play tourist and see what we can find out. If they are frequent flyers, the locals will know them. We have incentives for information. We will work that angle on our end. Abs, get a burner and send me the number, all off the books from here out."

"First thing in the morning. Shane, be careful.

"Keep in touch"

The line went dead. Crane and Adams stared at each other than the wall. This was real. It was happing.

| 20 |

CHAPTER 20

THAILAND

Harris and Phantom spent a few hours putting finishing touches on their plan. It wasn't grand, it wasn't pretty, but it was workable. Under normal circumstances they would have more than a two-man team, more resources, more intel, more of just about everything. They would have weapons. What they had now was years of experience, determination, one good contact, a few locals, some equipment thanks to Phantom, and they had a Leatherman. The go to of any operator, Boy Scout or guys guy. You could do a lot with the small do it all pocketknife. It was compact and had multi-functions. Most importantly, they could get it through most security points.

Their plan was to do reconnaissance, gather intel from locals, and find a place to hide for the night. Depending on what they found, they would regroup and revise. No part of the plan including direct contact or even being seen. They would move in the shadows, pay for discretion, blend in, play different parts and disappear. In and out, leaving no evidence they had ever been there. Not having weapons wouldn't be a problem. The plan didn't call for them, but plans are just that, theories, fluid thoughts and strategic thinking. Plans changed, were subject to human error, weather, unforeseen events, or even miscalculations. In other words, plans always change. Harris and Phantom would be ready for that. They were well trained and experts in just about everything that could go wrong.

They packed up and hit the rack for a few hours of shut eye. They would leave the rental house, turn in the car and catch the ferry. They wouldn't be returning here. After Phuket Island they would be on a transport home in two and half days. As far as Thailand officials were concerned, they weren't in the country anymore. Nothing could go wrong; they weren't even here.

Shane tried to quiet his mind; he needed to sleep while he could. It would probably be the last chance he got before he was on his way back to the states. The plan was as solid as could be. The gear was checked and rechecked. He memorized every detail they had unearthed. This was the first clue in Vanessa's disappearance since the day she went missing over a decade ago. He knew he was on the right path, he knew there was something here. He played every scenario over and over until he had a play for anything that he could imagine. So why was sleep being so evasive. He was exhausted, physically and mentally.

He took a few calming breaths, repositioned himself and shut his eyes. He pictured Abby, her slim figure, dark hair pulled back, hand on her hip, chew on the end of her pen. He thought of her miles away trying to piece together clues, sticky notes everywhere, push pins holding papers on the wall. He hadn't seen her in years, but when he heard her voice today, all the tension he was holding released. Abby always had that effect on him. She quieted the storm inside him, believed in him. When they were younger, she was the only one who understood his guilt, his pain, because she felt it too.

They met at a youth grief support group when they were teens. Both grieving the loss of their sisters, blaming themselves. They had leaned on each other when they felt the world stopped listening, stopped caring. When people quit searching for Daphne and Vanessa, Shane and Abby never did. They supported each other, drove each other. Shane always knew Abby would go into law enforcement, even when her father pushed her to go to law school. When Shane made the decision to join the military, Abby had worried for him, but she was proud.

Shane thought about how easily they fell into conversation, like time hadn't passed, like they just talked yesterday. Shane thought about her partner, Adams. It hadn't occurred to him before but it was late on her end. She said she was told to take time off, so she was home. Was her partner accustomed to spending late nights at her house? She obviously shares intimate details of Vanessa's disappearance with him. How close were they? Shane stopped himself before his mind spiraled. What did it matter? Abby was a grown woman. She was smart, beautiful, successful, of course she would have people in her life. Friends, partners, romantic interests. It was none of Shane's business. This was about Daphne and Vanessa. They were what was important, to Shane and Abby.

This is what Shane told himself as he drifted off to sleep. His dreams filling with images of Abby laughing, her brows furrowing when she was frustrated, the far way look in her eyes when she was deep in thought. The pride illuminating from her the day she took her oath to defend and protect.

***

After turning in the rental car, they caught a ride to the ferry that would take them to Phuket Island. It was cash only from now on and they would use passports with backstopped names. They were tourists, ad execs from LA, on vacation. They even had business cards from a business with a working website. The phone number would reach an automated answering service with several mailboxes in case someone entered more than the two extensions. It was enough for the few days they needed. No one would check, but if they did, they would get enough to make them seem legit. By the time anyone thought enough to do a deep dive, they would be long gone.

The ferry from Pattaya to Phuket was about five hours. Shane and Phantom took that time to study the maps they were given. The ferry would bring them into Rassada Pier. From there it would be a thirty-minute drive to Kata Beach, a location that came up several times in their intel. It would be their starting point. For now, they did their best to look like tourists, pointing, taking pictures, laughing. All the while they were taking in their surroundings, landmarks, people, the ferry, staff.

They made it to the pier late afternoon. They grabbed some food and a drink in a nearby market before grabbing a taxi to Kata. On the ride they did their best to be as unremarkable as possible. Talk, but not too loud or too much. Tip but not too little or too much. Nothing that would make someone remember you over every other Joe Schmoe that caught a ride that day. The ride was pretty quick and uneventful. Shane took in as much as he could without staring. Phantom was doing the same from his side. Abby had text him with a number for her burner. Good girl he thought. Shane gave the driver the address to a generic predetermined hotel.

When they arrived, Phantom paid the driver and they walked in the lobby. They waited a few minutes before walking back out, ensuring the taxi was already off with his next fair. The hotel they picked was in a central location, putting local restaurants and markets within walking distance in either direction. They were meeting a contact in a booth at the market half a mile away in forty minutes. That gave them plenty of time to get there and scope the area before the meet. Phantom's guy from the NGO had text a picture of the guy they were meeting. He vouched for him and said his information would be solid. The guy would be well compensated, no matter what he could give them.

They made their way towards the market. Blending in with the crowds, locals, tourists, families and couples. Even deep in conversation they took in every store, ally, road, cars parked or passing, people standing on corners, anything that could be of interest later. The market was easy to find. Mostly outdoor, covered booths, selling food, souvenirs, local handmade trinkets and items. After clocking all entrances and exits, Phantom found a nook between two booths near the meeting point, pulled up the picture and familiarized himself with the target. Shane found a similar spot on the other side of the walkway and did the same. They had the two-way radios to communicate, so for now they stayed in the shadows and waited.

After about fifteen minutes, Phantom spotted their contact. "Your two o'clock, blue shirt, black pants, black hat. Walking this way."

Shane glanced around from his hideout, spotting the older man about fifty feet away. "I got him. I'll let him pass, we'll pick him up at your twenty."

"10-4."

Shane watched the man pass him, looking for anything out of place. No weapons he could pick out, he seemed confident and sure of where he was going. When he was a good ten feet out, Shane fell in with the crowd behind him. A few feet later the man quickly disappeared into alcove. If Shane was aware it was going to happen, he wouldn't have noticed. Picking up his pace slightly, he slipped into the alcove behind the man. Phantom was already patting him down.

"Sorry 'bout this brother but we have to be careful."

"I understand. I am friend, I want to help. Do what you need to."

Phantom nodded to me that he was clean. The man turned, noticing Shane had joined them for the first time. The man held up his hands and nodded his head.

"You call me Joe, Ok."

"Ok, Joe. You can just call us friends. You know what we are looking for?" Phantom spoke softly but firmly.

"Yes. Ok. You looking for two girls. American. With another woman, a man and a boy. I was told you have a picture and names, yes?"

Shane pulled the picture from his pack, "These two girls are American but might not be traveling that way. They may use the names Viktoria and Natasha. We don't know the names of the others. Do you know anything about them?"

Joe took the photo and stared at it. He looked at both of the women. "I see them. Not American. Russian." Joe's face contorted when he said it, and he spit on the ground.

"Russian? Are you sure?" Shane asked

"Yes. Russians everywhere here. Driving up prices, taking jobs. Opening clubs. I see these girls with the Russian man and woman. They come here every few months. Usually only one of the girls at a time with the kids. The kids come here more. They might stay here longer. The girls only come for a short time. They have been coming for a few years. This one's hair is shorter now." Joe pointed to Vanessa's picture.

"Do you know anything else about them? Names? Where they stay?" Phantom was counting out money as he spoke.

"Thank you for this, but I would do it for nothing. These are bad people. There are condos not far off the beach. They have one on the top. My wife's sister cleans for them. Open's it up before they come. Takes care of things you know. She is very afraid of them but the money is very good."

"Can you show me where on this map?" Shane folded the map so that Kata Beach was facing them.

Joe studied the map, "We are here, see?" Joe pointed to indicate the market. "The beach is here; up this way is where the condos are. See here?" Joe pointed again.

Phantom circled the area with a red pencil. "Here?"

"Yes. But there is a gate, cameras that they see inside. You won't get in. And the doors have magnet locks. Even on the rooms. You need card."

The three men stared at the map, not sure what to do next.

"Let me make call." Joe walked to the back of the alcove. He spoke low and fast. He was obviously meeting resistance on the other end but was making progress. Shane made out some of it. "It's just money. These people are devils. What about your daughter?"

A few minutes later Joe turned back to us, "You understand, this is dangerous for us. But these people, they take our girls, our children. They ruin our way of life. They leave destruction. I will help you. You must be careful. There are other women and children there now. One you are looking for too. Meet me tonight, two blocks away here. I will give you what you need." Joe pointed to the meeting spot then bolted into the crowd.

Shane looked at Phantom, "Contact wasn't part of our plan."

"Brother, it's your sister. Fuck plans."

| 21 |

CHAPTER 21

FLORIDA

Crane and Adams spent another few hours working on the time-line. Using the information Shane had provided, Adams pulled some more information from the internet. Much of what they were able to find on public search engines matched with what they already had. Crane printed out maps of Thailand, focusing on Pattaya and Phuket. Armed with packs of multicolored sticky notes, they started putting together what they knew about businesses and Russian influence in those areas.

Satisfied they did what they could for the night, Adams left sometime after midnight. Crane felt a pang of guilt for letting him get involved in this at any level, let alone take him from his precious family. Crane me be on a forced vacation but her partner still had to work. Not to mention be a husband and father to two small girls. Crane knew those missing elements in her life were exactly what was driving Adams to help her. It wasn't that Crane didn't want children or a family of her own, she thought about, but then she opened another file and her trust in humanity washed those desires away. Crane couldn't protect her own sister, how could she bring life into this world, a life that would be completely dependent on her?

She could the stress of the day setting between her shoulders. Nothing more could be done tonight and she needed to sleep. She cleaned up the remnants of dinner and made her way to her bedroom. Murch followed, happily stretching out on the bed while Crane prepared the shower. She let the hot water run down her back, loosening the tension between her shoulder blades. She could feel herself relaxing, the day melting away. When the water started to run cooler, she turned it off, stepping out into the steamy bathroom.

Dressed for bed, Crane cuddled next to Murch and let herself relax. She made a mental list of what needed to be accomplished in the morning and let her thoughts drift. She thought about Shane, on his own mission, thousands of miles away. She rarely knew where he was at any given time, but she knew he had a team of highly trained men at his side. This was different. This time he had one man with him, a man she only knew as Phantom, in a country he wasn't really in. She didn't get to Shane often; their careers kept them busy. She tried to remember the last time she saw him. It had been several years now. They called on holidays, birthdays, anniversaries. When they couldn't call, they would email. Over the past few years, it had been more emails than anything. It didn't matter, Shane still felt like he was sitting right next to her. It never felt like they were growing apart, simply that life was moving forward.

Just hearing his voice silenced all the doubts she was having about this case, about herself. Shane renewed her confidence, grounded her. She believed in instincts again. They were onto something and together they would follow the trail through the depths of hell if that's where it took them. Crane only spoke to Phantom for the first time tonight, but she had already pulled him into her tight circle, adding him to her list of family and including him in her prayers.

Crane wasn't sure how long she had slept. Light was already creeping through the blinds. Murch was awake and ready to start the day. She wanted to pull the blankets up and sleep a few minutes longer but there was too much to get done. She sat up and checked her phone, hoping for an update from Shane. Then she remembered he was waited for her to text him with the burner number before giving her any more information.

Crane sat up, blinked the sleep from her eyes, gave Murch a pat on the head and got dressed. After downing a cup of coffee, she grabbed Murch's leash and headed out for a quick run. As they made their way through the neighborhood, she went over her to-do list in her head. She needed to call Agent Morris to give her an update and explanation for the late-night email. Not wanted to waste any time, Crane had sent the age enhanced pictures of Daphne and Vanessa with a brief explanation of what she needed. She didn't want to go into too much detail in an email so she needs to call. Then she needed to pick up a new phone and find out how Shane and Phantom were doing. She was worried about them more than she wanted to admit. Adams was going to look at the videos from the ICAC catalog had a thumbnail, Crane couldn't do that without logging into the system, which she couldn't do while she was in timeout. Hopefully Adams could get clean screenshots to printout and give her. She had never been so torn in her life, one part of her hoped she would find Vanessa in one of those videos, proof she had been alive, the other part hoping her sister wasn't subjected to that type of horror.

Back at the house, Crane called Agent Morris while she fed Murch and downed more coffee. She filled Morris in on everything that happened since they last spoke. Morris already started the passport search, but even with the parameters, wasn't hopeful she would have results anytime soon. Morris seemed relieved that Shane and I were in contact. Over the years, Morris, like Crane and Shane, had also believed both cases were linked. Morris had been the lead detective on Daphne Harris' case. She always believed Daphne had been abducted, but with no evidence and political pressure, she had been forced to close the case after the bloody shoe was discovered only months later.

When Vanessa went missing, Crane's father had used his influence to bring Morris in as a consultant. After only days working on Vanessa's case, Morris was even more convinced both girls had not only been abducted, but by the same person. Morris had come up against resistance with her theory, and again, with no evidence to back it up, the case went cold.

Now, Crane could hear the regret in her voice as she asked questions and verified information. Crane could tell, Morris was feeling she should have fought harder for Daphne and Vanessa. That she should have done more. Feeling that Crane herself had lived with for many years. Crane heard the grief in Morris's voice, grief that mirrored her own, and Shane's.

"This is good intel. I feel it. We didn't have access to this back then. You couldn't have known, we couldn't have known. You are the only one officially working this. I'm so far under the radar, I'm scraping treetops. And Shane, my God, he practically doesn't exist right now. We know what is on the line for us. We have been waiting for this moment since we were kids. You need to stay between the lines. I know you have a lot invested, but this isn't your fight, you don't need to go down in flames if it comes to that."

"Oh honey, I've been playing this game long enough. If this is the case that I go out with, I am ok with that. There is so much I can do here at DHS. So many more doors that are open that weren't before. Whatever can be done, will be done. The rest we will find a way."

"Shane wants me to get a burner, I'll text you with that number when I get it."

"Good idea. Keep me updated and as soon as I get anything I will let you know. Abby, we will get answers."

***

Crane showered, dressed and was out the door in thirty minutes. She purchased a basic phone with minimal capabilities from a box store near her house. Once it was set up, she texts Shane then Morris. She drove to a coffee shop down the street and grabbed some caffeine to go.

She sat in her car, phone in one hand, coffee in other, and waited. It was long before Shane text her a link for an encrypted messaging app with a calling feature. She quickly downloaded the link and called him.

Shane told her about his contact "Joe" and the intel he had given. He told her they were meeting up with him soon, hopefully he would have a something that would give him and Phantom access to the condo. She didn't have a good feeling about this.

"Just so I understand this correctly, you two met a random guy, who calls himself "Joe." This guy tells you he recognizes the pictures and names. Coincidently this stranger's sister-in-law is the housekeeper for the possible home of who you are looking for. He says they have a lot of security, he is afraid, then makes a brief, but heated call. Now he wants to meet you a few blocks from a condo with who knows what security, to give you something that might help you get in?"

"I mean, when you put it that way, it sounds a little ridiculous."

"A little ridiculous? How about, an ambush? A setup? You are defense-less and relying on a stranger for something you don't even know what!"

"Abbs, calm down. I heard part of the conversation. They have his niece. He was scared for her. He said one of the girls in the picture is there now! Do you get that? One of our sisters is blocks away from me right now!"

It took a few minutes for the words to sink in. She knew they were onto something; she knew her gut was telling her something was there, hiding under all the information, just waiting for her to see it. Something that would link everything together. But Shane was saying he was standing only a few blocks away from one of their sisters. Not a picture, not a video, but a living, breathing version of a piece of them. Suddenly it was all very real. A switch flipped inside her, going from rogue sister on a mission, to rogue trained investigator on a mission.

"Abbs, are you there? Can you hear me?"

"Yes. Did you say one of them is there now?

"That is what the sister-in-law said. One of the girls is there, that there are other girls too and children."

"The intel you have is that they only come every few months and stay for a week?"

"That is what two different sources have confirmed."

"OK. That's good. That narrows our search parameters Shane. Now we are looking for one of them that entered the country in the last week. That is huge!"

"Oh my God. I didn't even think about that. I got to go. Our guy will be here soon."

Ok. I have to call Morris. Call me as soon as you can"

The line went dead and she immediately dialed Morris.

"One of the girls is on Phuket Island right now. I don't know which one. So, narrow your search to both photos, the names Viktoria and Natasha, entering Thailand, Phuket Island, within the last week."

"That will narrow it down a lot. I should have something for you within the hour."

Crane made her way back home. She needed something to do while she waited. Morris was filtering through passports, Shane was getting ready to invade the unknown, Adams was searching through old videos, and Crane was sitting at home spinning her wheels.

Crane started going back through case files. Organizing witness statements, supplemental reports, forensics, evidence. Everything she had access to from both cases. Then she compared the stacks from each case to the other case, looking for similarities or overlaps. Something was nagging the back of her brain but she just couldn't pull it forward.

Her thought process was interrupted by text message from Adams. It was a string of still shots taken from the videos she asked him to review. She flipped through them one by one. About six pictures in, she saw it. Vanessa. She was wearing dark makeup and a girl scout uniform. Crane dropped her phone and started sobbing.

| 22 |

CHAPTER 22

PHUKET ISLAND

Shane hung up with Abby, smiling to himself at the berating she had given him. Hearing her put the plan into words did sound reckless, but what choice did he have? One of their sisters was feet away, he couldn't afford to trust local authorities to follow up. It could take weeks for government red tape to work itself out. He had no way of knowing what officials on this side could be trusted. By the time politics played out, they would gone, intel would be cold and he would be back in the US. He had no choice but to trust Joe.

Phantom had walked the perimeter of the property, eyeing cameras and security measures that could be seen with the naked eye. They had watched the entry gate for several minutes, noting vehicles either being buzzed in or using bar code stickers on windows. There were two pedestrian gates located at the front and west side of the property. Both gates required either an unknown number of digits numerical code or a magnetic access key card. No one had used those entrances since their arrival. The front vehicle gate and two pedestrian gates were approximately eight feet of vertical iron rods, spaced twelve inches apart. The rest of the property was enclosed by decorative block, approximately twelve feet high, hidden by shrubbery and vines.

Phantom had spotted two cameras at the vehicle entrance, one camera at each pedestrian gate, fixed cameras faces inside and outside the wall every ten feet. Joe had mentioned there were cameras that could be watched inside the condo. That could mean, residents had access to entry cameras to see who they were letting in, or whoever owned the condo had added additional security measures that utilized wi-fi. From their vantage point it was hard to get a good look without drawing attention to themselves. As it was, they were taking a chance walking around in daylight if someone was monitoring the area. They were careful, each making a rotation around the property, taking a map and a few brochures, they grabbed from one of the booths. To anyone watching it would look like to different people looking for any number of tourist attractions within walking distance.

They found a spot half a block down and across the street from where they were to meet Joe. They arrived early and found spots across the street from each other. If this was a setup, they would have a chance to see it coming. They planned exit routes and meet up spots if things got harry. They had coms and were alert. Any number of scenarios could play out here, but Shane felt Joe wanted to help. He was scared, he was nervous, but Joe was also fed up and needed help as much as he needed to help. Joe had left the market without taking any money. If he was setting them up, he could have easily taken their money too.

"Eight O'clock, he's alone. Let him wait a minute to be sure."

Shane found Joe walking up the path where Phantom had spotted him. He was walking quicker than he had in the market, looking around every few feet. Shane tracked him, watching his body language, checking corners and nearby vehicles. Nothing seemed out of place. Joe walked to the corner where they were to meet, looked around, walked down a bit, then walked back. He stood there for a few minutes then took out his phone. He flipped through a few screens, stopped on one, then put it back in his pocket. He hadn't messaged anyone or made any calls.

"It looks clear. I don't want to leave him too long. He might take off."

"Ok. I got the rear. I'll stay out of sight while you make contact."

Shane made his way toward Joe, taking a direct path. Joe saw him and looked relieved.

"Friend, I thought maybe you not come."

"I know how much you are putting on the line just being here Joe. I appreciate it. What do have."

"I'm so sorry my friend. My wife sister, she is so scared of these people. They would know if she gave up her key. She said it was just too dangerous. She wouldn't risk it. I begged her."

"It's ok Joe. I don't expect anyone to risk their lives. Do you have anything that can help me?"

"This." Joe pulled a folded sheet of paper from his pocket. He unfolded it to reveal a drawing. "This is what the inside of the condo looks like. My wife sister draw it for you. There are four bedrooms. They are marked here. Three bathrooms marked here. This is the kitchen and pantry. Here is important, it is an office. She says they keep papers for girls in Pattaya. The balcony comes around like this. You can get to it from the big room, eating room and main bedroom. These red marks are cameras. There are locks on all the doors. They use key cards, except the office, it has a regular key. She said one time during a storm, they lost power and the locks didn't work. Since then, they have a generator for when the power goes out."

"Joe this is all very helpful."

"Friend, I have more. Tomorrow, very early, the maintenance man, he will meet you at the side gate. He will take you to the electrical room. If you can figure out the power, he will take you to the room. From there you are on your own."

"Joe, this is amazing. Please let me give you something for your help."

"All I want is this," Joe took out his phone and opened up a screen. He turned it so Shane could see a picture of a little girl, about nine years old. "This is my niece. She is there. Find her. Get her out."

Shane stared at the photograph, memorizing every detail. "I will find her Joe."

"Bless you, my friend."

With a tear in his eye, Joe shook Shane's hand before walking away. For the first time since meeting May, Shane realized how many lives were affected by these people. How many sisters, daughters, nieces were missing, loved and mourned.

Shane made his way to where Phantom had posted up. He showed him the hand draw map of the condo. Now they had an exact location they could pick out the condo from the street. Shane went over what Joe told him.

"For fucks sake. What is wrong with people? These shitbags don't deserve to suck wind."

"We need to find higher ground so we can get a better look. I need to fill Abby in."

They found a hotel a few streets over. Phantom gave his speech about leaving his credit card at a club the night before, offering to give a hefty cash deposit if they would let him pay cash for the night. Sorting the details, he requested a room on the top floor facing northwest.

It was a request that would make them stand out later but in twenty-four hours they would be out of the country so it was a chance worth taking.

Shane grabbed some food while Phantom got the room. One memorable guest was better than two. Phantom text Shane the room number and thirty minutes later they were looking out the small window at the complex. There was no balcony but they had a better idea of the interior layout of the complex from this vantage point.

With the sketch of the condo and a bird's eye view, they hatched a plan for the morning over food and beer. Cutting the power and delaying the generator would be easy. Doing it in the early morning hours would draw less attention. The problem was they didn't know what was waiting inside the condo. None of the intel mentioned any armed security, nor had they spotted any. If there were armed guards, they would be inside, out of sight of other residents. It would still be dark when they went in, they had the Nods, so they wouldn't be blind giving them the advantage. If the cameras worked off Wi-Fi, cutting the power would take care of them too. Temporarily at least.

Going over everything, they would have ten minutes from the time they cut power to get in, grab what and who they could and get out before causing a scene. This couldn't turn into a firefight or draw attention. This was strictly a grab and go mission. They didn't exist here and getting caught wasn't an option. Not only would no one be coming for them but cost the lives of anyone inside the condo. If anyone knew people were coming for them, those in charge would destroy everything and everyone to get out.

The gravity of what they were about to do was setting in. Shane felt the strain of the lives in his hands. He thought about Daphne, Vanessa, about May, Joe's niece. There were so many people depending on him to get this right. He had no time to prepare, a team of two, and half a plan compiled of a shit ton of ifs and maybes.

"Puts a lot of shit into perspective don't it." Phantom stated more than asked.

"We know this kind of stuff happens. This evil exists. It hits harder when it's happened at your front door. To your family. When the faces have names."

"We won't stop until we get them. Not just your family, or Abby's, but the assholes who did this. This is personal. It's your family and you're my family."

They stood in silence, staring out into the night. Letting the quiet fill the room.

Shane put down his beer and picked up his phone.

"I'm gonna let Abbs know what's happening on our end and grab a shower."

"Tell Ms. Officer I said hey."

Shane sent Abby a text:

Met with Joe. Have a plan. Target a go in the morning.

| 23 |

CHAPTER 23

FLORIDA

Crane went from sitting on idle to high speed. Agent Morris got a hit. Hits to be exact. Crane was now staring at actual photographs of Daphne and Vanessa. Real images of two women, who until moments ago, were only children in her memories. The age enhancing program had been good, but it had not done the women's true beauty justice. Vanessa looked like their mother. Her hair was lighter, highlights framing her face, slender nose, high cheek bones, long neck. Crane imagined her grown up, tall and slender, still a with a ballerina's figure. Poised and graceful. Vanessa was beautiful. It was just a passport photo, but Crane could see parts of herself, her mother and her father staring back at her. She focused on the image, searching her memories, had she seen her? Passed her in the street? Would Vanessa know her? As beautiful as she was, her eyes were dull, missing the mischievous glint she had as a child. It was obvious her beauty was only exterior, a shell for the world to see. Crane couldn't see any hint of life, or her sister beyond her skin.

Daphne's photo was much the same. She was gorgeous, long flowing dark waves cascaded behind her shoulders. Her skin was fair and flawless. Her lips were full and tinted pink. She looked like Shane, she had his eyes, the same curve around the mouth. Her eyes were deep in color but just as hollow. There was nothing behind them. It was as if the girls had been constructed of porcelain, with painted glass eyes. Made to be put on display, to be admired, too delicate to be touched. Crane knew better, she had seen the evidence. She knew the girls had been touched. Touched, defiled, beaten, tortured, and raped. Crane felt bile rising in her throat.

She barely made it to the bathroom before losing the lunch she had forced herself to eat. Images of Vanessa and Daphne, their young bodies being used and mutilated, flooded her mind, making her stomach violently twist. She threw up until there was nothing left in her. Then she dry heaved until she was weak. Crane melted to the floor, resting her head on the toilet. She sobbed softly as Murch licked her tears away.

When she was confident, she could stand up again, she rinsed her mouth and splashed cold water on her face. She had to get a grip and focus on what needed to be done. Information was fluid and coming in quickly. Thanks to Morris and her team they Vanessa was using the name Natasha Broska and Daphne was using Viktoria Broska. A cursory look into the documents linked the women as sisters, with addresses in LA and New York City. The addresses were legit but it would take time to get rental and tenant information. Morris was working on getting copies of the documents used to obtain the passports. So far, they knew the passports had originally been obtained when both girls were eighteen.

Crane was sure they had passports previously and Morris was checking into that. It was possible they had different names then or different variations. The passports were issued from the United States and showed frequent visits to Thailand, France, and the Ukraine. The girls seemed to travel together most times which did not coincide with the information they received from multiple sources in Thailand. They had not found any US passports for children with that last name but were still searching. They also had negative results for older men or another female traveling to the same locations or during the same time periods with that last name. Morris was working on variations of the last name, hyphens and surnames.

They were able to confirm that Viktoria and Natasha had flown out of Hartsfield-Jackson Atlanta Airport (ATL) to Phuket International Airport (HKT) five days ago. Morris was searching for booking for returning flights now. They weren't able to trace any connecting flights prior to Atlanta. This part didn't make sense. If Vanessa was residing in LA and Daphne in New York City, why did they fly out of Atlanta together with no previous flights? Had they already been in Atlanta together? Did they drive across country to meet in Atlanta to take a flight? If they had driven, were they in danger? Were they still being held captive or had they started new lives?

The more answers they found, the more questions Crane had.

Crane was relieved that Shane's meeting with Joe had gone well. She had been worried for hours waiting to hear from him. She had envisioned a Wild West shoot out in the middle of a narrow street in the middle of a Thai beach town. Shane and Phantom walking down the sidewalk, unassumingly waiting for their new confidant, when suddenly men jump out bushes, cars and from behind buildings, mowing down her friends in a hail of bullets. It was dramatic, but she had been sitting around doing nothing while everyone else was busy chasing down something.

Crane didn't idle well. She was high strung by nature and needed to be doing something. Her sister's disappearance was a huge part of her life. It had forever altered the course of her destiny. Now, a decade later, her course was changing again. Upheaving everything around her, rocking her foundation to the core. She couldn't talk to her mother about this. Not yet. Vanessa's abduction devastated their family. Then when Crane's father had passed away so suddenly, she didn't think her mom would ever recover. But she had, she pulled herself up and started living again. Crane couldn't pull her into this and be wrong. She couldn't do that to her mother. Morris had her hands full; Adams was working and Shane was off the grid. Crane had reached out to Mr. Petrov, the man who had led their grief support group years ago. She had kept in touch with him over the years and he still ran a group a few towns over. She hadn't been to a meeting since she left for college but she had fond memories of those weekly sessions where she could talk and be heard.

Mr. Petrov had lost his daughter many years ago, long before she and Crane came around. Mr. Petrov was a substitute teacher and photographer. He started a grief support group to help him get through the loss of his daughter. Seeing how families were affected in different ways, he realized siblings of lost loved ones needed a safe place to gather and talk freely with other kids struggling in the same way. Morris had brought her to the meeting and Crane was glad she had. Morris had done the same for Shane. Those meeting were how they met, and they had been kindred spirits ever since. Mr. Petrov let them talk, helped them put their grief unto words and gave them perspective of what their parents were going through. She had been grateful for his guidance then and could really use it now. She had gotten his voicemail, leaving a message to call when he could. Crane had decided to email him in case he was in class. She had explained that there were developments in her sister's case, real information, and she was having trouble processing it. Just putting in writing had helped her immensely.

Crane's phone rang bringing her back to reality. Instinctively she grabbed her phone and answered, "Crane." She was greeted by nothing but silence. She heard her phone ring again, confused she looked at the screen but it was black. Feeling like an idiot she realized it was the burner. She followed the sound, looking under papers and pillows, until she found it hiding under Murch's tail.

"Thanks for the help bud." She gave his ears a quick scratch before answer the phone for a second time, "Crane."

"Hey, I got them on a flight leaving tomorrow, late afternoon, 1955 their time, flying into New York, JFK arriving 850 the next morning."

"Is it a direct flight?"

"Uh... No, looks like there is a few hours layover in DOH, Qatar."

"Ok, not likely they would get off and stay there."

"No. No history in that area and not exactly the kind of place two females would stop off."

"So, this is good news? Should Shane just observe and let them leave?"

"It's good. We are already putting a team together in New York. We will be able to control things on the ground. We don't if they are traveling alone or what the situation is. They will have to clear customs, that will be our window. We can have our agents pull them for a random screening. It happens all the time so it won't draw any suspicion."

"So, Shane can just follow them to the airport and make sure they get on? That is the safest thing?"

"Normally I would say absolutely under the circumstances."

"But?"

"But we have a very rare opportunity to obtain operational records on a trafficking ring that has been in business for almost twenty years. Working in multiple countries. If he can get in and grab any records, we have a chance of not only getting the girls back but of bringing these people down."

"I don't like this. He's risking a lot when we can get the girls here. I'm already looking at flights to New York now. I am going to be there."

"I wouldn't expect anything less. Abby, you have to understand, this isn't just about Vanessa and Daphne. You saw the series ICAC was able to put together. That is just what they have so far. This goes back to the late 90's. That's hundreds, maybe thousands of children. Children that are still in danger. Abby, you have to remember there is a bigger picture. Shane is a big boy, he knows what he is doing."

Crane looked at all the pins decorating her living room wall. She thought of all the images she saw every day at work. All the daughters, sons, sisters, brothers, all those innocent children waiting for someone to come rescue them from the monsters that are all too real. She knew Morris was right. Opportunities like this rarely, if ever, presented themselves. A lot was at stake, no matter what they did.

"Ok, I will let him know."

Crane hung up with Morris and opened the messaging app.

She pulled up Shane's last message and replied:

Girls are booked on flight out of HKT 1955 your time tomorrow. Morris needs info you can get hands on. Grab and go. B safe.

She attached the passport photos and closed the app. Next, she called Adams and filled him in on the progress they made. She told him she was booking a flight to New York and asked if he could take Murch for her. He said of he would, the girls would be elated to have their pal for a sleepover. He would stop by afterwork and pick up his fury friend. Crane thanked him and started gathering her pup's necessities for a few days away. For a dog, Murch traveled heavy, he had his away orthopedic bed, leash, toys, tennis ball, treats, food, bowls, and blanket. Sensing her dismay at his ever-growing pile of essentials, Murch sat by the door, tilting his head left then right, before giving her the biggest puppy grin ever.

"You're lucky you're cute."

***

Adams picked up Murch who greeted his pal with whines and tail wags. Crane barely said goodbye before he jetted out the door to Adams sedan. Her partner wished her luck and handed her hard copies of the stills he had emailed her earlier. She hugged him tight and thanked him for everything. She was lucky he was her partner.

Crane was barely packed when her phone started ringing. She raced to the living room to answer it, grabbing the call just before it went to the voicemail box she hadn't bothered to set up. "Crane."

"We have a problem." Morris sounded anxious and out of breath.

"Oh God. What's wrong?"

"We found the departing flight quickly because it had be made as part of a round-trip booking."

"Ok"

"I had the passports flagged and they hit. They already left Phuket. The departed on a semi-private jet four hours ago from HKT"

"Semi-private?"

"It's a private plane that can be leased out to multiple passengers. The flight manifests are last minute but the passports had to be scanned because they were leaving the country."

"Do we know where they are going?"

"That plane is going to Doha in Qatar. From there they could be taking another private or a commercial to anywhere. We don't know why the sudden change. Have you heard anything from Shane?

"No not yet. He should be getting ready to hit the place anytime now. Do you think he was burned?"

"I don't know, the timing is odd. They will be landing in about two hours. We will have a better idea of where they are heading next then. Hopefully it's still to the US."

"Shit. I this doesn't feel right. First, they are together which we are told doesn't happen. Then they fly out of Atlanta when one is in LA and the other is in New York. Then they have flights already, returning to New York not Atlanta, but are whisked away on a private plane in the middle of the night? What the hell is going on?"

"Hold on." Crane could hear a muffled conversation in the background. "I'll add to the what the fuck bucket, we have them on a flight out of Doha coming into Miami. You have a bag ready?"

"Yea, I was packed for New York already."

"Cancel that flight. I'll pick you up in a few hours. We are heading to Miami. They land in eighteen hours. Doesn't give us much time to put something in play. I have so calls to make. I'll text you when I am on my way. Have coffee ready."

"Always."

Crane hung up and pulled Shane's contact up again.

Change of plans. Girls left four hours ago. Inbound to Miami eta 18 hours

| 24 |

CHAPTER 24

PHUKET ISLAND

Phantom was up first. Checking the gear, batteries, function, mentally checking things off his list as he packed them away in his pack. Timing was going to be tight so everything needed to assessable and functional. The plan was hasty but workable. He looked over at the kid, finally still after jerking in his sleep all night. Phantom could only imagine the terrors wreaking havoc on his brain. This could be career ending for both of them, if not life ending. The team knew about Harris' sister from the start. They had no secrets from each other. They knew how hard the kid had worked to overcome the dark place he went to after his sister disappeared. They all loved him. One thing the team didn't know was, Phantom was a product of rape. His mother stayed the night at a friend's house after a party when she was a senior in high school. Her friend's father had given them wine, treated them like adults. Later that night he had come into the bedroom and raped Phantom's mother on the floor while his own daughter lay passed out on the bed. His mother had been so ashamed she hadn't said anything. The families had been friends for years.

When she found out she was pregnant, she finally told her parents. They didn't believe her, accusing her of lying to coverup a one nightstand with a boy they didn't approve of. They kicked her out of the house and her friend refused to speak to her. It was years later, when Phantom was ten or so, that the truth came out when the guy's niece ended up pregnant at thirteen. It took time, but eventually his grandparents and mom made amends. They never talked about it though. More or less just pretended those years didn't happen. As Phantom got older, he distanced himself from that part of his family. His mother may be able to forgive and forget, but he couldn't.

That's why he had told Pop there was no way he was leaving Thailand without knowing if the kid's sister was here. Finding out how many children were involved in sex trafficking, how many families were damaged by this growing industry, he knew he made the right choice, that he was in the right place doing what he was meant to do. No matter how this went, he had no regrets. He spent his adult life fighting wars for other people for a plethora of reasons, many honorable, some not. This war was his, it was personal, it was worth fighting, and the people he was fighting it for were defenseless, innocent and voiceless. He couldn't think of anyone more worthy of a savior.

Shane was waking up, shaking the sleep from his bones.

"Mornin' sunshine."

Shane replied with something between a grunt and a groan. He was on his feet and dressed in five minutes. He began his own equipment checks and crosschecks. Mentally checking off his gear list as he put things in his go bag. Once he was sure everything was where it needed to be he checked his phone. He read Abs message and pulled up the attached photos. He was frozen in place, in time, staring at the face of a stranger that was both familiar and unknown at the same time. He hadn't seen Daphne since she was ten years old, but he would know her anywhere. He always wondered what she would look like all grown up. Her hair was still long and dark, her skin fair. Her eyes were the same almond shape as his. He saw his father's jawline and his mother's nose. The likeness to the AI depiction was uncanny. But the real-life photo was stunning. His sister was beautiful. She was real and she was alive.

"What's Ms. Officer got to say?"

Shane turned to phone so Phantom could see.

"Oh shit. She looks like you bud. I mean like you but better. Certainly, makes things real, don't it?"

"It sure does. I never thought I would get to moment. I never thought I would see her grown up in anything other than a computer enhancement. I knew it was her right away. What if she doesn't recognize me?"

"A bridge we'll cross when we get to it. Just focus on getting to her."

"Abs says they are booked on a flight out tonight at 1900. Looks like it's go time."

"Do or die brother, do or die."

They gathered their stuff and headed out. Everything going as planned, they would be back on the mainland by evening and on a transport home in the morning. No matter what happened, they had to be on that flight, it was their only way back into the states. Shane had already made peace with this being a one-shot mission. Ten minutes, grab and go, back to the mainland. Daphne may not be one of the things he can grab. He was going to do whatever he could to make that happen, but if he couldn't, he would get whatever intel he could, whoever he could, and get out. They knew where the girls were going, when they were going, if he couldn't get to them, they had another chance. As hard as it would be, if he had to, he would have to leave her behind.

Phantom and Shane talked about what was VIP and what was negotiable on the way to the property. Phantom shared his feelings about Daphne and Vanessa. Now that they knew where they had been and where they were going, they had more to work with. They would have other opportunities where time would be on their side if it came to that. Getting into that office and getting any documents they could find was a one-time shot, getting the other kids was essential. Grab and go, ten minutes, in and out.

It was still dark out with minimal street lighting. They seemed to be the only life stirring in the wee hours of the morning. They made it to the west gate, avoiding any surveillance cameras they saw. When they approached the gate, a young man, around twenty, partially hidden by the shrubbery, greeted them.

"You friends of Joe?"

"Yes. We were told you need help with a maintenance problem?"

"Yes, put these on. I take you where you need to be." The kid tossed two blue collared shirts with a company logo of the breast pocket.

Shane and Phantom threw the polos on over their shirts and followed the kid through the gate. They made their way through a maze of sidewalks and covered walkways before coming to a door marked "Employees Only." The kid swiped his key and they slipped inside. Lights flickered on as they made their way down a long corridor. They passed doors on each side that were marked as offices, storage and stairwells. Near the end of the hall, they made a left turn taking them down a shorter hall. Halfway down was a door marked "Electrical." The kid swiped his card again and they ducked inside.

Once inside the kid turned on the lights and sat his bag down. "No cameras in this room so we can talk. I will show you the panels and the generator. Over here is map. It's for emergency paths but I can show you how to get to the top floor."

They walked to a wall with a large board covered with posters, schedules and clipboards. The kid handed each of them a clip board and told them everyone on property carried one. It would look more official. Next to the board was the map of the property, The kid pointed out where they were now, then indicated where the closest stairwell was. He showed them that they would use that one to go up to the third floor then cross over the corridor to get to the opposite stairwell. From there they would go up two more flights. When the exited the condo would be the second door on the right.

The kid confirmed there were two independent cameras on the exterior of the condo. One facing down the hall towards the elevator and the other facing the door itself. When they exited the stairwell, they would be in a blind spot for about fifteen feet. The cameras were hardwired and not Wi-Fi. He didn't know of any other security measures.

Next, he showed them the generator that the property had installed for backup power. It was a standard commercial generator used to provide minimal power. They didn't have time to work the wiring to disable it. The kid told them it kicked in fairly quickly. That didn't work for them, they would need time. Phantom picked up a wrench from a toolbox on the bench. After giving the main panel of the generator a look over, he used the wrench to smash the panel. Then he pulled a few wires out, disconnecting something from somewhere. At the very least, it would slow start up process.

"Sometimes brute force works."

Shane shook his head and the kid tried to hide a smile as we moved on to the main fuse panel. This would be an easier process. All we had to do was find the main power shut off to the building. There were four buildings and with any luck they were labeled and we would be able to find the right fuses.

Of course they weren't in English, nor were the laminated cheat sheets hanging from the panels. The kids English was decent but trying to explain what we needed slightly complicated things. This wasn't something we could be fairly certain about and we couldn't risk one of us going outside. This couldn't be a guess and hope for the best type of situation. After a few minutes of debating and pointing, we put on our Nods and just flipped all the switches. Everyone was going to lose power for a bit, but at least we knew we disabled the right one.

Seconds later the lights went out and we were in night vision mode.

"Go time"

Phantom made his way down the corridor first, Shane taking up the rear. Quick but steady, moving with purpose, heads on a swivel. They took the stairs two at a time, making it to the third-floor landing without breaking a sweat. They eased their way into the corridor. Quick, steady, purposeful, head on a swivel. So far so good. No one seemed to notice the impromptu blackout. They reached the second stairwell without incident. Slowing their pace, evening out their breathing, preparing for what came next.

Phantom cracked the door open, looking into the hall. He spotted the cameras, the red lights glowing in the darkness. They were inferred. They had expected this, even prepared for it. Shane followed closely behind Phantom, staying as low as possible. They reached the edge of the blind spot, about five feet from the door. They took out the Leathermans from their pockets. Each were equipped with penlights in red or green. Twist the top left for green, and right for red. The thing about infrared cameras is they adjust to the light around them, if its bright they work in day mode, if its dark, they are in night mode.

In night mode the camera adjusts color saturation much like a filter to accommodate the lack of natural light. Pointing a red beam directly at the cameral while in night mode confuses the sensors, essentially blinding it.

Shane pointed his light at the camera covering the hall, and Phantoms at the one over the door. Phantom moved forward checking the door. The magnetic lock was disabled and there didn't seem to be any other mechanism in place. Phantom eased the door open, listening for any sounds on the other side. When he was sure it was clear he gave Shane the go ahead. Shane put away the penlights and stacked up on Phantom. He tapped three times on Phantoms shoulder then they made entry, Phantom pushing the door open the swinging right against the wall. Shane followed, swinging left around the door. Once inside, Shane eased the door closed. They were in the foyer, the dinette and kitchen on Shane's side and main room on Phantoms. The balcony was on Phantom's side, meaning the master bedroom was at the end of his wall and the office on the other side of the main room. The other bedrooms and bathrooms were on Shane's side. They quietly maneuvered forwarded toward the office. As they moved, they could see the master bedroom door was closed.

They checked each bedroom, which were empty but recently used. They reached the office next. It was locked. It took Shane thirty seconds to get in. As soon as they opened the door, they felt sea air on their skin. The balcony door was open and they could smell something burnt. They made their way further into the office, on the balcony was a large trash can filled to the top. It was still smoldering. Shane looked to the side at the large desk. Drawers hung open, empty, a pile of paper clips and rubber bands on the floor. A safe hidden in a cabinet stood open, also empty.

Phantom followed Shane's eyes, both realizing what happened, hurried to the balcony. Phantom kicked over the trash can, sending ash and debris into the air. Whoever burned the documents was in a hurry, haphazardly throwing everything in the bin, shoving it all down then lighting on fire. Most everything on top was reduce to soot, but the stuff on the bottom had blocked airflow, stifling the flames before they could burn. Shane grabbed anything that looked salvageable and threw it in his bag.

Someone knew they were coming. This wasn't good.

They worked their way back into the main room to the master bedroom. This time Shane took the lead, throwing open the door, entering quickly. Frightened cries came from a corner on the opposite side of the room. Phantom and Shane made their way over, clearing corners and closets as they went. Huddled in the bathroom were seven girls, different ages in varying stages of undress. They were scared, some beaten, one unconscious. Shane did his best to tell them he was there to help and everything was going to be okay. Phantom ripped the sheets from the bed, wrapping the young girls.

Shane checked his watch. They were out of time. They had to get out of here, now. Daphne and Vanessa were nowhere to be found but they couldn't wait. Phantom checked the unconscious girl; she was breathing and had a weak pulse. He scoops her up while Shane herded the others out of the condo and down the stairs.

It took a few minutes longer to get out the gate with the extra baggage. They made in a few blocks away and ducked behind a building. They took off the shirts the kid had given them and Shane called Joe. He told him he found his niece and other children. He gave their location and told him to hurry. He told him he had to be on the first ferry to the mainland, even if it meant leaving the children behind. Joe said he would be there soon and would bring help.

Phantom was on the phone with his contact with the NGO. Explaining what the found, the condition of the children, asking if they could contact anyone to help. Phantom told him they were never here and couldn't do anymore. They spoke for several more minutes. Phantom fell silent, then hung up. He crouched down and hung his head, staying like this until Shane stood beside him.

"Joe is on his way with help. They will take the kids until they can get more official help. He will keep us out of it."

"My guy is working on getting people here. He knows Joe. Kid, there's something else. They fished a body out of the canal by the Walking Street in Pattaya. Its May. I'm so sorry."

Shane turned away, balling his fists until his knuckles were white. He had done this to her. Maybe not directly but if he had left her alone, she would be alive.

As if reading his mind, Phantom stood up and put a hand on his shoulder, "This isn't on you. She was a dead girl walking the day those bastards took her from her village. You didn't do this.

Look at those babies over there. You saved them. You did this."

Shane looked at the girls, tears streaking their faces. Sitting together, wrapped in a sheet. Shane wondered if they understood they were really safe. He imagined they had been told everything would be okay many times, then it was everything but.

He checked his messages and saw he had another one from Abbs. And punches keep coming.

"Abbs says the girls boarded a private plane a few hours ago. They are Miami bound. She and Morris are heading that way."

| 25 |

CHAPTER 25

FLORIDA

Crane was on her second cup of coffee, pacing from her living room to her kitchen and back again, when Morris finally arrived. They now had fifteen hours before Vanessa and Daphne's flight landed at MIA. It was a four-hour drive in the best traffic conditions. Best case scenario they would have eleven hours to develop, organize and execute a plan at one of the busiest and largest international airports int the country. At least they had a four-hour drive to talk it. Unfortunately, it was one in the morning, meaning they wouldn't be able to get ahold of anyone until they were there. That also meant the flight was arriving four in the afternoon, rush hour traffic and peak arrival departure times. The city and the airport were going to be a madhouse.

I showed Morris where I kept my travel mugs, creamer and the freshly brewed pot of coffee. While she made us caffeine to go, I grabbed my bag and files. When I came out of the bedroom she was standing in the living room, staring at my newly decorated wall. I had added more to my timeline and sticky notes were everywhere. All that was missing was colored string connecting all my notes and pictures. Then I would have an official who done it wall. To an outsider it probably looked like nonsense, but to me it was organized chaos. I had all the pieces; I just haven't figured out how they fit together.

"It's pretty impressive. I might higher you when I renovate my living room."

"Ha! I call it workaholic deco."

"Seriously. It's impressive. You put a lot together quickly. All this from an off handed comment in an interview. Those are instincts you can't teach. Those you are born with. You should be proud of yourself. I know your father would be."

"Even though I didn't go to law school and become a Supreme Court Justice?"

"Even though. He knew you had a calling. He just didn't want what happened to Vanessa to consume you, to dictate your future."

"I know. It's funny how things work out. Shane chose the military to take him as far away from his past as possible, I chose law enforcement to make peace with mine. Somehow we both ended up in the same place anyway."

"We call that fate where I come from."

We threw my stuff and ourselves into Morris' SUV and headed out. It reminded of the drives she would take me on as a teenager. Little outings to get me out of the house, check in on me. We would talk about everything and nothing. It made me feel included in the investigation, in the search. Like I was a part of it all. That was so important to me back then. Here we were thirteen years later, driving to Miami, making feel included all over again.

"I keep going back to my timeline, to the cases files. Something is pulling at the back of my brain and I can't figure out what it is. Each new piece of information we get, the hard it gets to shake it free."

"The mind is funny that way. The harder we try to see something, the more distorted the picture becomes. You know those pictures where you have to unfocus your eyes to see it? Like you look at it and you see one thing, but if you unfocus your eyes and look at it a different way, you see something completely different? Cases can be like that too."

"Like the picture of the hourglass that is really two people facing each other?"

"Exactly. Then once you see it, you can't image how you ever saw it any other way."

"Then there is the whole flight thing. All our sources say the girls never visit the Island together. They both come every few months for a week. They are either accompanied by an elderly man or another female. Then when they are on the Island they are seen with a boy. Not boys but a boy. Like it's the same boy. Then we follow their travel history on the passports and find they mostly travel together, several times to the Island together. Never with any children, boy or girl, and we haven't linked this mystery elderly man. Now we have one living in LA, the other living in New York, but they fly out of Atlanta? Again, together? Is it just me or are we missing something?"

"No, you're right. It isn't adding up. When we went back through the passports, they fly out of different international airports. Sometimes New York, Atlanta, Orlando, Miami. Why not fly out from where they live? They both have international airports. We still have some searches to do but so far, we aren't finding any other flights. No connecting domestic flights or other domestic travel. We have put in requests with the IRS and Social Security for tax and wage history. So far, no hits on any social media. No hits on those names other than the passports and ID cards for home states. No driving records, licenses, or criminal histories. We are still waiting on the passport application records to get birth records, social security numbers and any other records submitted."

"It's like they turned eighteen and emerged Natasha and Viktoria. We know they have been together for at least nine years from the timeline I put together. If I had to bet, I would say they have been together since Vanessa was taken. Most of the girls who have series, I can place in similar outfits and backgrounds for a short period of time. One girl, who I believe is the first girl, I have her for several years. The same with Daphne and Vanessa, between the photos and videos, there are about two years. Why the quick turn over with the others but keep these three? I can't get over the feeling we are missing something huge."

"Me too. I went over other missing children reports, five years prior to five years after, and nothing close to the same circumstances. There are a lot of abductions, some where they just disappeared and never seen again, but I didn't get the same feeling from those. Something about these two has always felt intentional, planned, precise, to me. I don't know, maybe I'm looking at an hourglass hoping to see two faces."

They fell into a comfortable silence, mulling over what laid ahead. Crane took out her phone to see if there was any news from Shane. Nothing yet. She checked her other phone checking for any messages from her mom or Adams. She had a text from her partner, picture of Murch stretched out on the couch with two of the cutest kiddos using him for a pillow. He looked content and the kids looked thrilled. She checked her email and saw the Mr. Petrov had responded. He was sorry he missed her but he was teaching all week. He told her to give it to God and he would be praying for her family. He could be reached after five if she needed him. He was such a sweet man. There was a voicemail from her mother, just checking in, call when you can.

Crane felt a little guilty keeping her mom in the dark but it was for the best. She knew that.

About an hour outside of Miami she got a call from Shane. She put him on speaker and he filled them in on what happened at the condo. He told Morris he was able to salvage some documents but they were in some code and in another language, maybe Russian. He would scan them to her as soon as he was state side then mail her the originals. He was on his way to the mainland to catch his transport back. He told them about the children, so young and scared, beaten and bloody. He had taken photos and scanned them with ABIS. Hopefully that would aid in identifying the kids or help identify traffickers. Shane's voice grew heavier as he told them about the discovery of May's body. He didn't have any other details for them yet.

Crane filled him in on what she and Morris had discussed. Told him they were going to be there when the plane landed, the plan was to stop them at customs under the guise of a random security check. It was the easiest way to seclude them in case they were not alone, get them away from prying eyes, and get them to safety before anyone realized what happened. Shane said he would be in the air by then but to leave him a message as soon as they could. He would call them when he landed at home. They said good luck and goodbye; both filled with worry for the other.

***

The airport was a zoo. Everywhere you looked, lines wrapped through mazes of queue ropes. People weighing luggage, redistributing clothing and re-weighing. Others standing in security lines, hopping on one foot trying to take of shoes, emptying pockets before stepping into body scanners. Lines of people getting last minute snacks or souvenirs. People and lines everywhere. Plain clothed agents were placed at the arrival gate, baggage claim, and numerous checkpoints along the way. Undercover agents were on standby at customs waiting to step in when the plane landed. Morris and Crane were seated in the security office watching a wall of TV screens displaying several views of varying areas of the airport receiving arriving international flights.

Homeland Security was working this with the help law enforcement assigned to the airport and airport security. It was a small-scale operation and they didn't want to many irons in the fire. The team was small but they were looking for two females, traveling alone, whom they would be able to isolate without incident. The more people involved the more that could go wrong. They didn't have much time to prepare but there wasn't much to prepare for. Crane was confident they would have come to the same conclusion if they had a week to prepare. Morris wanted her to have eyes everywhere, thinking Crane was their best hope of recognizing the girls.

Crane knew the reality was, this was Morris' op and Crane was here as a personal favor. Crane had provided pertinent intel and Morris felt guilty. Crane had no jurisdiction here, had no jurisdiction with the case, she was no more than a civilian bystander. Morris was doing her a favor letting her come along and putting her in an office watching TV screens was the easiest way to make sure neither Crane nor Morris' career became an unnecessary casualty. Crane appreciated all of it. Vickers giving her time off, Adams getting her files, Shane putting his life on the line and Morris putting her career on the line. She felt loved, she felt Vanessa was loved. She hoped it would be enough.

Suddenly radios came to life with chatter. The guy in front on the screens started pressing buttons and moving a joystick. There was activity at the gate. Agents started checking in. Everyone was in place and ready. The plane would begin disembarking anytime now. The joystick operator zeroed in on the gate door, waiting for it to open. Everyone was quiet, waiting for the doors to open. Crane scanned the screens trying to pick out the agents at their stations. There was a lot of traffic in the corridor. Two other arrivals were expected, one came in a half hour earlier, then the one from DOH, another expected twenty minutes later. It was a tight window, but manageable. Crane was still scanning the corridor thinking there was a lot of people around, more than she thought there should be when more radio traffic started.

"Plane is taxied in and ready for disembarking. Already starting to unload luggage. Should be any minute now."

Crane knew first class would be the first off, and the girls were in coach. Another thing that struck her has odd; they take a private jet then fly coach?

"Slight commotion in customs with a kid but working it out. We'll be ready."

The doors opened and passengers started making their way through the gate, some checking to see which terminal they could retrieve their baggage at, others walking straight through. Several families with very pale skin passed through the cameras view. Something seemed off about these passengers. Just as Crane was asking joystick guy to pan out to the plane, someone came across the radio again.

"We've had a change in baggage claim. That second flight from Europe arrived early and has our Doha baggage. Doha was moved three lanes down. People have already started collecting."

About then Crane got a view of the plane which was not the airline flying out of Qatar.

"Somebody verify what gate our plane is at!"

"Can you give me a visual of the area around arriving flights? Where would they exit from?"

Joystick guy punched a few buttons and pulled up a new panel of camera views. I scanned them as fast as my eyes could process them. Three screens in, going up an escalator I spotted to slim figures holding the hands of two small boys. Both women with dark hair just below their shoulders, heads low with large sunglasses.

"There. Where is that? That's them."

"That's out the door, straight down then a left toward the exit. Door E, I think. Near the taxis."

Morris was standing next to me looking at the women move up the escalator.

"My god. The flight was earlier and was directed to a gate on the other side."

I was on my feet and out the door before Morris could tell me to stop. I heard her voice yelling after me, then radios cracking. I didn't wait to hear what was said. Better to beg for forgiveness than ask permission, or something like that. They had let them slip through the cracks thirteen years ago. Again, two days ago in Thailand, and for the last time twenty minutes ago. Crane wasn't going to let it happen again. She wasn't going to let Vanessa down again.

Crane saw the ladies step off the escalator heading for the exit. They were a good distance away, closing on the exit. Crane started to run, dodging people and luggage. She was gaining on them but they would hit the exit before her. She broke into a full sprint, when she was within earshot, she yelled as loud as her winded lungs could, "Nessy!"

Both girls turned, glancing over their shoulders. They were at the exit but Crane was closing in. One of the females grabbed the smallest boy in her arms, taking the other by the hand. Both women took off, cutting between waiting cars. A dark SUV with tinted windows came to a stop in the far outside thru lane. The women saw it at changed direction heading towards the rear passenger door that had swung open. Passing cars swerved and honked as the females made their way across traffic. A male arm reaches out from inside the vehicle and the boy ran towards him, jumping in the backseat.

Crane was so close, traffic had separated the girls, slowing one of them down. The first female made it to the car, throwing the smaller child inside. The second female caught up, it looked like they were struggling to both get it inside or with each other. The second female wedged herself between the SUV and the door. Using the SUV as leverage she kicked the other girl with both feet, knocking her backward away from the vehicle. The woman jumped inside slamming the door and the SUV sped off.

Crane was almost to the second female who had gotten back on her feet. Crane didn't understand what just happened. She was two lanes away from the stunned girl who was stumbled and turned towards her. Just then a car moved from the standing lane, crossing two lanes to get around vehicles that had stopped to watch the spectacle.

Crane heard the screeching tires, smelt the burning rubber and brakes. The car hit the woman as she turned, sending her onto the hood the crushing the windshield.

Crane felt the blood rush from her as she ran towards the crumpled body.

"NOOOO!"

Crane managed to tell someone to call 911. Agents started surrounding her. The girl was alive, but with all the blood, cuts and swelling Crane couldn't tell which sister she was looking at.

EPILOGUE

It seemed like hours before the ambulance arrived. They loaded the fragile figure on a gurney and sped off to the nearest trauma center. Morris found Crane and they met the ambulance at the ER. Because they weren't sure which girl they had, she was being listed as a Jane Doe. A flock of doctors and nurses had gathered around Jane, evaluating all her injuries. Within minutes she being rolled into surgery and Crane was being ushered into the waiting room.

Morris set up round the clock security for Jane. Hospital staff was made aware of the situation. Morris listed Crane as member of the security team and a liaison contact. It was the only was Crane would be able to stay with Jane and be updated on her condition until her identity was confirmed. Jane's injuries were extensive and surgery took hours.

Morris brought food and a change clothes. They waited together, sitting, not speaking. Crane left Shane a voicemail. She wasn't even sure what she said or if she made any sense. She had decided not to call her mom until she had definitive news. Time was standing still; Crane's heart stopped every time the door opened. The waiting was killing her.

Seven hours later a doctor finally emerged. There had been internal bleeding, a broken hip, broken clavicle, broken jaw, and swelling in the brain. They had inserted a drain to elevate pressure but they wouldn't know the extent of the damage for several days. Jane would be kept in a medically induced coma to give her body time to heal.

Additionally, there were several older wounds, bones that had been broken, showing various stages of healing, different signs of trauma consistent with long term abuse. They were moving Jane to a private room in ICU to accommodate the security detail.

Once Jane was settled, Crane was escorted in. She stared at the broken body, hoping to recognize something. Her face and body were so distorted from injuries, tubes, and tape, she barely looked human. Crane had a DNA sample taken and ran against Daphne and Vanessa's profile. Morris had put a rush on it so they would know soon enough. Either way, one of the girls was home. They would start getting answers.

Crane didn't have a chance to review any surveillance video of what transpired at the airport, but it just added to the accumulating pile of strange events. Tomorrow was another day, today was a day for rest. Crane found a blanket in a cabinet and curled up in small recliner next to the bed.

Crane slept for hours, not even waking when the nurses did their hourly checks. An agent woke her taping her with a manilla folder marked urgent.

"DNA results. Morris told the lab to bring them straight to you."

"Oh, thank you. I was expecting these."

"No worries. Any news?"

"No change yet. Doctors say she will be out for a few more days."

"Well, she's in my prayers."

The agent left and Crane sat up. She turned over the envelope and started pulling open the seal. Her phone started ringing, she looked at the caller ID and saw it was Shane.

"Hey, you've got good timing, I was just opening the DNA results. Give me a sec."

Crane worked the seal and pulled two sheets of paper out. The top sheet was the testers letter, an explanation of testing procedure and qualifications. The second sheet provided the results. Crane read over them, tears falling from her eyes. She began sobbing so hard it rocked her body.

"Abbs? Abbs? What's wrong? Abbs?"

"Shane, you need to come, please come."

Author Bio

From a young age TR Cliborne was an avid reader, devouring as many books as possible. She loved the feel of the pages in between her fingers and the way her mind transformed her surroundings into castles, battlegrounds, dungeons, or schoolyards. With a book in hand, she could go anywhere her imagination could take her.

When Cliborne was in high school, she was drawn to writing, creating her own heroes and villains, towns and cities, weaving together plots and storylines. She tried her hand at poetry and even song writing, but found fiction was her forte.

TR Cliborne strayed from her love of writing to explore a calling to serve. She joined the US Army Reserves, serving for six years. She met her husband while serving in the military, marrying three years later. While serving in the reserves, Cliborne sought out a career in serving her community as a law enforcement officer.

During her career in law enforcement, she worked in patrol, as a Field Training Officer, and a Detective in different areas. One of these assignments was with the Internet Crimes Against Children (ICAC) task force. Cliborne felt this was her calling and worked cases involving crimes against children for several years.

While cross training with the Mounted Patrol Unit, she suffered a catastrophic injury, hospitalizing her for several months. After months in and out of the hospital, in patient and outpatient therapies, and multiply surgeries, she was unable to return to work and medically retired.

Retirement from the career she loved sent her looking for fulfillment. Cliborne found that again in writing. She uses her knowledge and experience to develop compelling crime thrillers with relatable characters and a unique perspective into the investigative world. She is the author of the Crane & Harris series, a breakout debut crime thriller.

Cliborne holds a BA in Criminal Justice Administration and Management with a minor in Psychology. She holds certificates in Criminal Profiling, Physical Security and Sex Offender Behavior.

TR Cliborne resides on the East coast with her husband who still works in law enforcement, her daughter, three dogs and smug cat who gives her much inspiration for her villainous characters.

Acknowledgements

I would like to thank my husband for his support, understanding, and the thankless hours he puts in serving out community. Especially for the time he dedicated to continuing the battle against crimes against children as a member of the ICAC task force.

I also owe a debt to azn_american and Dr Jon B for their insights, feedback and continued support. Without them, Shane Harris and his team wouldn't have come to life or conducted such compelling operations. As always, thank you for your service gentlemen.

Unconditional thanks and love to the members and volunteers of the many organizations and NGO's that are on the front lines, battle the monsters, and making the world a safer place for our children.

For more information on how you can volunteer or help fight crimes against children, visit any of the follow sites:

Ourrescue.org

Thorn.org

Covenantrescue.org

www.missingkids.org